OCEANAUTS

ALEXANDER DUBBELS

To my father, who encouraged me to come up with an original story.

CHAPTER 1

In a world where humans and anthropomorphic sea creatures coexist, there was once a town called Sandy Shores. Here, humans went about their lives in harmony with lionfish, anemones, urchins, salmon, and lobsters, and the ground was covered in sand.

The town was built on a seashore, hence the name, and inland was majestic wilderness. Red, green, and yellow trees. Beautiful ferns with blue, brown, and green berries. Root vegetables, red, orange, yellow, and white. Wild eggplants, spinach, and edible mushrooms galore.

In the center of town, there was an apartment building. This apartment building accommodated one such denizen, a human named Niko. Niko was a sort of inventor/innovator and used his small apartment to house all his contraptions. He was constantly working on clothes that society would wear to give them special abilities. He was very close to a breakthrough, having modified gloves the wearer would use to lift things off the ground. However, due to lack of funding, his inventions were mostly unsuccessful.

On the day which our story begins, Niko's dainty apartment was particularly messy, littered with technology, action figures, and canned food. Niko was overdue on rent. His job laid him off and his landlord, a dolphin named Percy, was not very soft. He had given Niko three days to pay rent. And today was the first day.

"I'm a failure," he told himself. "I can't make a simple invention. I just don't have the materials, time, or money. If I could, I'd be rich! But I can't, and I'm not. I guess it was never meant to be." He got up and walked to his desk in his bedroom. He sat in his chair and stared at the gloves that lay there. "These gloves are perfect. And yet I have the feeling nobody will want to buy them."

He stared at them. After a moment, he slipped them on.

"And of course, I'll be able to give you a good apartment," said Percy. He was conversing with a guest at the front desk in the lobby. "For the right price, of course." He handed the guest a room key card.

Thumping was coming from upstairs. Percy groaned. "Another one of Niko's infernal contraptions again?" he muttered.

"Are you talking to me?" asked the guest.

"No."

"Okay. It just sounded like you were."

"Well, I wasn't. I have to go. There's a certain problem I must sort out upstairs."

"Got you."

"Bye!" Percy ran into the elevator and pressed the fifth-floor button. He grumbled to himself. Niko's antics had caused his building more physical and financial troubles than any other guest he had ever housed.

Niko was lifting and maneuvering things through the air using the gloves. He was cleaning and organizing his apartment. The room was presently spotless and tidy.

Percy burst in. "What's going on in here?" he demanded. His voice shook like thunder as he spoke.

Niko froze. "Uh, nothing." He removed the gloves from his hands and shoved them in a drawer.

Percy charged into Niko's bedroom. His eyes widened when he gazed upon the well-organized splendor before him. "Why..." he began to say.

"Why what, sir?" asked Niko.

"Why..."

"Why...?"

"Why, for once in your life, this room looks absolutely splendid!" He leaned in close. "What's your secret? A professional cleaning team that climbed in and out the window in no time at all?"

Niko shrugged. "You could say that."

"Absolutely splendid, Niko! I thought you were an unholy mess, never cleaning any filthy thing you create! How did you manage to clean this room in practically no time at all?"

Niko smiled. "Let's just say I had some help from one of my inventions."

Percy's eyes widened larger. "Do you mean to say one of *your* worthless contraptions cleaned this place?! That's crazy!"

Niko sighed. "We are all full of surprises, aren't we?"

Percy returned to his normal state. "Yes, I suppose we are. Do you plan on coming down for lunch today? I'm cooking up a real treat for everybody!"

"What is it?"

"Stuffed biscuits."

Niko sighed happily, "I love stuffed biscuits! Thank you!"

"You are most welcome, and don't forget to leave a tip on the table for good ol' Percy!" Percy laughed a hearty laugh and exited the apartment, heading for the elevator.

Niko peered out the window. The sun hung high in the sky. It was about 11:02 in the morning and the streets of Sandy Shores were bustling with citizens and transport. Niko sighed once more and hopped into his bed. He laid down and pondered his many thoughts. *I don't get it. I just don't get it. Why did he have such a sudden change in heart over my inventions? He's been a qualified enemy of mine since I moved in here.* Niko sat up straight in bed. A new thought struck him with a dash of horror. *Does he think he can sneak in here, steal them, get a phony patent, and sell them?"* He got out of bed with a jolt. "I don't think so."

Niko walked over to his desk and slipped a combination lock on the handle of the drawer he kept the gloves in. "Phew! All my fears for today are over. Time for lunch." He started to his bedroom door, then stopped. "Except for one thing…"

How would he pay for the apartment?

You see, Niko was a man of ingenuity and resourcefulness. As bespoke, he was very inventive and innovative. He worked night and day at whatever he set his mind to. He salvaged materials from the local junkyard anytime he could (which was nearly all day because of his lack of work), meaning he was perpetually chock-full of any supply. And because his apartment was small, with very little room for his rapidly growing number of supplies, it was made dirtier and dirtier. Percy was infuriated at this and gave Niko a three-day warning instead of the usual week. On top of it all, the family below Niko said an odd green liquid was seeping out of their ceiling vent covers. Niko was blamed for this, even though he swore he had nothing to do with it.

As he made his way down to the first floor for lunch, Niko wondered how he would pay Percy for the apartment. He knew, even if he got a job today, there was no way he'd rack up enough money. If there was one thing Percy liked more than monochromatic chess, it was negotiating a deal involving money. Niko knew Percy would have studied law if he could afford it. There was no way he could strike up a deal that would make enough sense to Percy for him to give him more time. Percy knew his stuff.

Not only did Niko try to find enough supplies for inventing in the town junkyard, but he also searched for buried treasure, gold coins and the like, but he didn't have any luck. He needed help.

Lots of it.

He entered the dining room on the first floor and picked up a paper plate, then scooped a generous helping of baked beans and one stuffed biscuit onto it. As he sat down at an empty booth, he couldn't help but know, deep down, he was doomed.

CHAPTER 2

Meanwhile at the squid mines…

At the squid mines, dwarf giant squids mined, the perfect people for the job. The squids were mining for coal and iron, two very important minerals for Sandy Shores. Squids were chosen for mining for three reasons: their gelatinous bodies weren't easily harmed by stray pickaxes (or any sharp object, for that matter), they could see in the dark, eliminating the need for head lamps, and their suckers could grip the ground they were standing on and the pickaxe they were holding. They could even walk up walls and ceilings of caverns if need be.

One such squid was Cawyer (pronounced like Sawyer). He had a desperate wish to be a foreman, even an assistant, but the current foreman, Spike, didn't think he had what it took.

That day Cawyer was hanging out in the break room with his colleagues. What was called the break room was really a clearing made in the cavern wall. It housed an old-timey box television set and a coffee table with beer and potato chips. Several squids were playing canasta. Others took part in pool. Some enjoyed watching football and hockey on the television.

Spike walked into the room. "All right, you guys! We've got a quota to make today and not too much time to do it! I'm expecting another cavern cleared by the end of the week! Time for another two hours of work!"

"Oh, all right," said Cawyer, groaning. Though the groaning was not because he disliked his job. Sadly, Cawyer had very little to do every day, save an occasional game of foosball in the break room. He only groaned because his job was very dull and repetitive. He longed for more excitement in his life, though a sort of cycle began. He'd come to work, do his dull job, yearn for excitement, come home, read a horror/mystery novel, and wonder if excitement was really worth all the trouble.

Although he gave the worst wake-up calls, Cawyer secretly admired Spike. His set ways and get-it-all-done-now mindset kept this mine running. Without Spike, it would be an abandoned mineshaft within the week. This was why Cawyer wanted to follow in his footsteps and why Spike didn't think Cawyer had what it took. Cawyer just wasn't tough enough and his mind often drifted. Speak of the devil...

Cawyer struck the cold, lifeless stone with his pickaxe for the next two hours. Every impact between metal and rock sent rattling to his body, which would rattle his spine if he had one. As Cawyer struck, he thought of his friend, Niko. Niko was his only company most days because none of Cawyer's relatives lived close by. Cawyer knew Niko had recently been laid off and was in financial troubles. Cawyer wasn't, so he gave Niko a generous third of his leftover money after all the bills were paid.

The squid mines—and all other mines in the area—had a certain system. If a miner found an extremely valuable or beautiful jewel, they would be allowed to keep it. However, the chances of that happening were extremely slim.

Cawyer had told himself millions of times that if such an event occurred, he would take none of the cash brought in from the gem and give it all to Niko. Besides, he was doing well. Niko wasn't. He had a steady, however dull it may be, job. Niko didn't. Besides, it wasn't as if he had a will or trust fund he could put it in. He could only imagine what the news anchors would say if Niko bought an extravagant Victorian mansion or something like that. "I owe it all to selling my inventions," he might say. Cawyer giggled under his breath. He didn't care if he didn't get any credit. Though he did wonder how overwhelmed Niko would be if everyone in Sandy Shores wanted to buy or invest in his inventions.

Cawyer's daydreaming was interrupted when his pickaxe hit something that answered with a *ting*. Confused, Cawyer peered to get a closer look and saw a shiny object. He slid the end of his arm over it. The odd thing was sharp and metallic.

Cawyer gasped. He knew what this meant.

It meant Niko wouldn't need so much of his income anymore. It meant Niko wouldn't need a job for months. Best of all, it meant Niko would be, for the first time in three weeks, happy.

"YAHOO!" Cawyer jumped for joy all around the cavern. "I wish I had my tap-dancing shoes!"

"Keep it down over there!" shouted Spike.

Cawyer calmed down and mined around the gem. He discovered it was approximately the size of a beluga whale. He couldn't believe his eyes. "This is amazing!" he muttered to himself. He proceeded to mine the entire thing out of its place. His pickaxe swerved out of control and hit the jewel itself. It shattered into a million pieces. "NOOOO!" shouted Cawyer. He became horribly angered and gripped his pickaxe tightly. He screamed at the top of his lungs and smashed the ground. Suddenly, he fell seven feet down into the hole he had just created.

"Cawyer!" Spike shouted. He marched up to the hole and looked down into it. His voice reminded Cawyer of a drill sergeant. "Stop fooling around! Have you forgotten the number-one rule about mining?!"

"No, sir."

"Never mine straight down!" He huffed and walked off.

Cawyer sighed and used his suckers to climb out of the site.

After getting over his horrible disappointment, he peered at the site and saw the crystal was really a thin pane between him and a large, hidden cavern.

Cawyer gulped and used his suckers to safely climb down into it. Once he got to a place he could stand on, he was approximately fifty feet from the hole he had made.

He looked around. He was standing on a dusty stone platform. But the stone was a bit odd, more evenly laid than simple rock. "Is that stone… bricks?"

He looked to the side. There was a sort of railing on either side of the platform. Looking over the railing, he saw a drop into a dark ravine. The platform extended on to a structure holding a shining object. The walls were lined with crystals. "This platform must be a bridge to that structure." He started for it, believing it may be an extremely valuable crystal, then paused. "If this *is* a bridge," he started, "then how do you enter? There's no door on this end that you can use to come out onto the bridge. Or are you supposed to come out of the hole I made? Were the builders cephalopods that could use their suckers to come down here, like me? Did they seal up the cavern with that crystal pane so nobody would find the place?" He shook his head. "That's too many questions for one squid to answer. I'm going to investigate the case myself."

He adopted a sophisticated stance and walked slowly across the bridge, taking note of stone gargoyles here and there that seemed to be breathing fire. "Interesting." He found his way to the end of the bridge, where the large structure stood. Cawyer walked up stairs, finding a gazebo-style roof above his head, supported by quartz columns. Inside the structure lay the most beautiful blue crystal he had ever seen. "Unbelievable," he whispered. "And it's perfectly cut, too!" He reached out to touch it.

"All right, time to go home!" shouted Spike. Cawyer winced. *I can even hear him from here!* "Drop the picks! Let's go!"

Cawyer sighed, set down his pickaxe, and left the mine. "This is so unfair," he told himself as he began the long ride home on his bicycle. "Now someone else is going to collect that crystal."

No one was left in the mine when a dark, large, ominous creature wearing a head lamp emerged from behind a boulder. "If only you had known how right you were, my friend," it said in a hoarse, menacing voice.

CHAPTER 3

The next morning…

Cawyer woke up immediately to the sound of his alarm clock. After brushing his beak, he sprinted outside, got on his bicycle, rang his bell three times for good luck, and rode toward Niko's apartment building.

Once Cawyer got there, he dismounted his bicycle and headed inside.

"Stop!" said the receptionist. She pasted on a sincere smile and asked, "What is your business here?"

"Uh," said Cawyer. "I'm here to see Niko Winchester Finnigan Jenson Percival—"

"Yeah, yeah!" exclaimed the receptionist. She looked very annoyed. "We both know who you're talking about." She had heard that name when Niko had first moved in and was not eager to hear it again. "Enjoy your visit."

"Thank you, ma'am!" Cawyer ran into the elevator and pressed the fifth-floor button. Once he arrived at Niko's door, he ran up to Niko's apartment and rapped the end of his arm on the door.

Niko was thinking hard. He knew today was his second day and, despite his efforts, couldn't get any money all the day before. He pulled the gloves from their drawer and pondered their ability. That's when he heard a knocking sound on the door.

"Yes?" answered the voice from inside as he opened the door.

"Hi, Niko!" said Cawyer.

"Cawyer! What a pleasant surprise! Please come in!"

"Thank you!" replied Cawyer as he stepped inside.

"By all means! It couldn't be that my best friend isn't allowed in my house!"

"Your apartment," Cawyer corrected.

"Ah, yes, well… I'm hoping I can have a home of my own one day."

"I might be able to be of some assistance in that area."

"Oh?"

"Yes! I found a gem in the squid mines yesterday that looked particularly valuable."

"Sweet!"

"If I get to work soon enough, I can claim it before my co-workers do!"

"That's great!"

"Well, come on, then!"

"What do you mean?"

"You're coming with me."

"Oh, no. I kind of thought you were going to go to work, collect it, and bring it to me after work."

"I thought it would go quicker if you came with me and got it yourself."

Niko couldn't argue with that. He checked his watch. Already 10:00 in the morning. With the deadline he had been given, he wasn't very confident. "No time to waste, I guess," he told Cawyer, and stuffed the gloves he was holding in his pants pocket.

"That's the spirit!"

They headed out of Niko's room and into the elevator. In no time at all they were in the driveway of the building. Each hopped onto their own bicycle and rode off into the rising sun, like in an epic movie.

Percy saw the two ride off through his office window. "What are those two up to?" he asked himself. "Has Niko finally grabbed hold of a steady job?"

"This is almost too good to be true!" said Niko.

"And so easy!" said Cawyer. "I thought this process would be finished over a period of months! But it seems it won't be that way!"

Niko remained silent.

"What's wrong, buddy?"

"I'm just worrying."

"About what?"

"Well, suppose it's not as easy as it seems. Suppose the crystal you found is not what it seems. Suppose it's targeted by an international smuggling ring, and we're riding right into trouble! Or—"

"Niko, Niko, Niko. Always worrying. It's going to be fine! Trust me, if that gem is targeted by some international smuggling ring or whatever you said, they wouldn't have been able to find it anyway. The place was closed at the end of the day, and I can tell you firsthand that unless you're a squid, angler fish, lantern shark, electric eel, or desperate criminal with a head lamp, you won't be able to find it."

"But what if somebody already owns the crystal? Wouldn't that mean, by taking it, we would be stealing private property?"

"Listen, Niko, it will be fine. Trust me. The worst that could happen would not being able to find it. Have I ever let you down?"

"Um…"

"No. Everything will be fine."

"Oh, very well. I suppose I should stop worrying."

"As bespoke, that's the spirit!"

They soon arrived at the squid mines. Spike was at the entrance waiting for Cawyer. "There you are!" he exclaimed. "Where were you? Don't you know we've got a schedule to—" his gaze drifted to Niko, "-keep. Ahem! What do you think you're doing? Only workers allowed!"

"That's not fair!" exclaimed Cawyer. "He just wants to look around! Surely that can't hurt!"

"We must keep the miners' code, Cawyer."

"But—"

"It's okay," said Niko. "I can wait out here."

Cawyer hung his head. "Oh, all right."

"Goodbye, Cawyer."

"Goodbye, Niko."

Cawyer headed inside. Niko sat on the floor next to his bicycle and waited for Cawyer to come out with the crystal.

Meanwhile, Cawyer grabbed his pickaxe and got to work. He mined into the opposite wall of the hole he had made yesterday. He collected a bunch of coal and one fleck of iron. He quickly looked around to make sure no one was looking. "I reckon I've collected enough minerals as a cover story." He snuck over to the hole he had made, took another quick look around, and climbed inside.

Niko soon got restless. He walked up to the mine and peered inside. He couldn't see a thing. He chuckled to himself. "This reminds me of looking into a window by day. I can't see inside, but the miners can see outside." He knelt to get a closer look. "Cawyer?" he whispered through gritted teeth. Finally, he'd had enough.

Niko stepped inside. He felt the cold stone wall to get a better sense of direction. He looked around. Though he couldn't see a thing except the entrance, he knew no one was looking at him. He knew they would immediately call out something like, "Hey! You're not supposed to be in here!" He slinked to a shining light. Looking closely, he saw it was the hole Cawyer had gone through, shining with the reflection of the crystals inside. He leaned a little too far in and fell.

Cawyer headed down to the stone brick bridge by using his suckers to climb down. As he walked along the bridge, he looked at the crystals lining the walls. "Today's the last day I'll be seeing you," he told them. He heard a sudden thud behind him. He quickly spun his head around. "What the what?"

CHAPTER 4

"Hi, Cawyer!" said a familiar voice. It sounded a bit strained, as if the voice's owner was in pain.

Cawyer spun his head around and widened his eyes in shock. "Niko?! What are you doing down here? Didn't Spike say not to—"

"Yeah, yeah, I heard what Spike said. I just thought I'd accompany you when we get that jewel!"

"Don't you care about your own good?"

Niko shrugged. "Spike's your boss, not mine. I don't have to listen to him."

"Isn't this a crime punishable for up to seventy-five years in federal prison? Can't you get arrested for entering private property without permission?"

"It's not really private property. I mean, tons of people have access to this place," Niko corrected. "And it's not like that's going to be any worse than my current situation. Maybe the contrary, even."

Cawyer couldn't argue with that. "All right, fine. You've got a point. Now come with me."

"Will do." Each of them began walking forwards and carefully stepped over a tripwire placed there, strewn between two railings on either side of the bridge, which wasn't there before.

"It's right over here," said Cawyer, pointing to the structure at the end of the bridge.

"Right over where?"

Cawyer gasped. "It's gone!"

Both friends gasped. This was unexpected.

"How?" Cawyer asked himself. He touched the structure columns. They were cold. Cawyer sighed.

"Where is it?" asked Niko.

"It's gone."

"Gone?"

"Yeah, gone. One of the other miners must have taken it. I'm sorry for getting your hopes up, Niko."

"It's okay, Cawyer. It's not your fault. You were late already, remember? One of your co-workers could have gotten it a billion years ago!"

"Yeah, yeah. I should stop beating myself up. Let's go."

The two walked along the bridge in silence. Cawyer extended a leg, nearly tripping the tripwire, then quickly retracted it. "No, Niko! I do owe you! I'll make it up to you if it costs me my life!"

"I have an inkling how, no pun intended."

"How?"

"You could mine out one of the gargantuan crystals embedded in the cavern ceiling? Ten to one it'll be just as much worth."

Cawyer slapped his forehead. He hardly knew now what had gotten him so worked up in the first place. "You're so right. I'll do that."

"Great! Thanks!" Niko ran along the bridge. And, in doing so, tripped the tripwire. "Whoa!" he shouted, tumbling to the ground. Cawyer watched in horror as the tripwire snapped.

Suddenly, the bridge beneath them began to crumble apart.

"Uh oh," said Niko. He had activated something.

One second, it was fine. The next second, the bridge was in a million pieces and Niko and Cawyer fell into the dark abyss below.

"I'm sorry for being so greedy!" shouted Niko, though he couldn't see Cawyer anywhere. "This is all my fault! I followed you in here! I tripped the tripwire!"

"You weren't greedy!" Cawyer shouted. "You were just desperate, that's all! I was the one who acted all—" SPLASH!

Suddenly, the world went dark and wet. Niko fell unconscious. Cawyer splayed out his arms, then pushed them inward, and repeated the motion until he reached the surface. He looked around. "Niko!" he called. "Niko!" Then it hit him. "Oh no." He dived under the water.

"Niko!" he called. It was a bit harder to see under the water. Cawyer dived deeper and saw Niko drifting away. "Niko!" He took Niko's hand with one of his arms and pulled him to the surface.

"Whoa!" sputtered Niko, gasping for air. He looked at his friend. "Cawyer, you saved my life!" He began to tread water.

"Oh, it was nothing."

"Thank you!"

"You're welcome." Cawyer, though he was trying to hide it, was extremely sad. "This is horrible," he muttered to himself.

As horrible as he felt, his uneasiness at stewing in his own guilt told him Niko was experiencing it ten times worse. He was the one who had gotten Niko's hopes up. He told Niko he could pay off that apartment and possibly become famous for his inventions by funding them with the money. Cawyer promised him that gem, and he let him down. Oh, well. Maybe something good would come of their current situation.

"Is our situation hopeless?" asked Cawyer.

"Nah, I don't think so. This water isn't still. We're moving, see? There's light up ahead."

"Phew!"

And escape they did. Their water ended in a grand waterfall that hurled them over the edge of a giant cliff, into a small pond at the bottom.

"I don't think we're going to make it out of here alive!" screamed Cawyer.

"Yeah, that small pool can't save us from fall damage."

They both screamed. SPLISH!

And that was that.

THE END.

"No!" said Niko. "It's not over! We're still alive! We'll never give up!"

Oh?

They both climbed out of the small pool, drenched and bruised, but still able to run any races.

Niko looked around. In front of them was an extensive forest of mixed trees, such as oaks, maples, birches, and ashes. Niko looked behind them. The rushing waterfall was still gushing water into that small pool. It came out of a majestic cliff. No sign at all of Sandy Shores.

Niko rustled Cawyer. "Cawyer, wake up!" he said. "We're still alive!"

"We are?"

"Yeah, but we're lost."

"Figures." The two stood up.

"And guess what?"

"What?"

"Look!" He pointed to a row of bushes. Among the bushes was the crystal, literally right there! It was obvious someone wanted to hide it in the bushes, but part of it was still poking out. They looked at each other. Was it really going to be this easy?"

CHAPTER 5

"You do the honors," said Cawyer.

"Are you sure?" asked Niko.

Cawyer shrugged. "Totally. You're the one who wanted it in the first place, right? I was just your errand boy."

Niko scoffed. "Well, I wouldn't call you an errand boy."

"No time to waste! You have a deadline, remember?"

Niko glanced up to the sky. Judging by the sun, it was about noon. "You're right." He walked up to the bushes and parted them, then gasped. "Oh no," he whispered. What they thought was just part of the crystal poking out of the bushes was only a shard of a crystal, possibly of *the* crystal. However, this was a vital clue. It meant the robber had come here.

"What's wrong?" asked Cawyer. He ran up to Niko. Niko showed him the shard. "Oh no," he breathed.

"Is there any clue as to where the robber might have gone?"

"Yes." Cawyer pointed to the floor. Tracks.

"No."

"Yes."

"You're kidding."

Great tiger shark tracks. Tyrant of the seas.

After a moment of silence, Cawyer said, "Scary, dude."

"It is," agreed Niko.

"But what can we do about it?"

"Well, we can't find our way back to Sandy Shores and we don't have a lot of other options, so…"

"You don't mean…"

"Yes. We're going to chase after him."

Cawyer's eyes widened. "But we haven't prepared for this trip one bit! Plus, we'll need something inhumanely strong to fight off a great tiger shark!"

"So that's one thing on the 'plus side'." He chuckled slightly. Cawyer frowned at him. He winced. "Well, we don't have a lot of other options."

Cawyer sighed. "As always, you're right. I can't argue about that. But we're no match for a great tiger shark!"

"Oh, yes, we are. We'll use my inventions!"

"Inventions? But your inventions are back at your apartment! Aren't they?"

"Oh, no!" He pulled his gloves out of his pocket. "I always carry successful inventions around with me, just in case the need to be an entrepreneur arises."

"So, your invention is successful?"

"Yep. First one in all my life that was."

"What do the gloves do?"

"I'll show you." He lifted the crystal shard with his gloves.

"That's amazing! It looks like something you might find in a graphic novel or science fiction movie!"

"Well, truth is stranger than fiction."

"It reminds me of the book Roald Dahl wrote called *Matilda*."

"Okay, it's time to go!"

"We should take inventory first."

"Good idea."

"I've got a pickaxe and two quarters."

"I've got these magic gloves and a slice of carrot cake."

"Where did you get a slice of carrot cake?"

"The pond." He pointed to the pond, where all sorts of goodies were around.

"Look!" said Cawyer. "It's that compass that points not to north, but what you want most!"

"That's convenient." He pulled the compass out of the water and held it high in the air.

"Where is it pointing?"

"That way!" Cawyer pointed to the forest.

Niko shrugged. "That's what I suspected anyway."

"Shall we leave now?" asked Cawyer.

"No. I have a feeling we might need this at some point." He pulled a small bike pump out of the water.

Cawyer shrugged. "Whatever you say, Niko."

"That's all. Let's go!" And, hand in hand, the two marched off into the forest, ready to claim the thing they wanted most.

The going was tough at first. Niko and Cawyer thought it was going to be a quick trip. You know, go there, get the crystal, come back, spend a night trying to find their way back to Sandy Shores, and sell the crystal so Niko could afford to pay Percy and fund his inventions. But they soon discovered it was going to take longer than they thought. Niko was holding the carrot cake in the sky with his glove and was forced to hold his arm up to do so. If he let go of the cake, it would fall to the floor and SPLOT, resulting in a less than appetizing meal. And they couldn't afford to lose this slice, as it was their only food. However, his arm soon tired, and he was forced to decide: stay like this or carry it with his hand? He couldn't set it down. They would need it on the journey. It wasn't going to walk with them. He couldn't put it in his pocket. It would smudge and the frosting would melt off. He couldn't give it to Cawyer. Cawyer's hands were full due to carrying his pickaxe and the compass.

"Urgh!" he groaned.

"What?" asked Cawyer.

"Nothing." He didn't want to sound like a wimp. And so there was silence. And then…

"Urgh!"

"What?"

"Nothing."

Silence.

"URGH!"

"What is it, Niko? You're obviously groaning about something. It's slightly harder for me to read the compass when you're groaning."

"Sorry, Cawyer. I can't help myself. It's too hard for me. The load's too much. The burden I cannot carry."

"What's too hard for you? What load is too much? What burden can you not carry?"

"This carrot cake!" He set it on the ground. They both paused walking for a second.

"Should we take a rest?" asked Cawyer.

"No!" said Niko. He began waving his arms around. "Vampires might come and attack us at night! We must find a place to sleep!

"Niko, vampire bats live in South America! Plus, I don't think they suck human blood, anyway."

"Cawyer, I didn't say vampire bats, I said—"

"Shush! If I'm here, no vampire squids will dare come and get us."

Niko sighed.

CHAPTER 6

"Let's make camp here. You go find some wild berries to garnish the carrot cake while I make a tarp and a campfire."

"Alright." Niko clambered off.

"Watch out for mountain lions!"

"There are mountain lions here?"

"Heck if I know! I've never set foot in a forest farther than my grandma's backyard!"

"Look, I'll be careful. Bye."

"Bye." Cawyer got to work. He stripped the trees of their leaves and all the big leaves from ground plants. He sewed them together using vines as thread and the antenna of a large beetle as a needle. Then he strewed the "tarp" over bare branches and got to work on the campfire.

He reaped the ground of grass using his pickaxe to create a nonflammable clearing. Then he began to pile sticks in a single spot. A fox came up and started sniffing around. "Hello, little guy," Cawyer said to the curious canine. The fox whined. "You're kind of cute." He rubbed his neck. The fox gazed earnestly at the stick Cawyer was holding. "Want to fetch boy?" He wagged the stick around. The fox's eyes followed it. "Go get it!" Cawyer threw the stick as far as he could. The fox ran to it. After ten seconds went by, Cawyer slapped his forehead. "Ah, how could I be so clueless? Foxes aren't tame; they don't know how to fetch!" He ran as fast as he could in the direction he had thrown the stick.

Niko climbed down a steep slope, carefully but hazardously, to make it to the valley below. His heart was beating quick, and his breathing was heavy. He was sure he would die if he wasn't careful. It was a twenty-foot drop from the cliffside to the valley below. Niko didn't have any climbing gear. One wrong step, one misguided grab, and that would be it for him.

Once he got to the bottom, Niko looked over at the forest before him. It was colorful and clean, no pollution in sight. Red, green, and yellow popped against the sharp contrast of the brown trunks below them. Green grass, sweet berry bushes, and rhododendrons sprouted from the ground. Daffodils, dandelions, and daisies littered the forest floor. "Here goes nothing," said Niko, stepping into the wooded wonder. He immediately began searching for wild berries.

"Where are you?" he asked the berries to be found. He got on his hands and knees and brushed aside twigs and leaves. An acorn weevil scurried up on a branch and gazed at him, then ran into the woods.

"Ah-ha!" screamed Niko. "I just said a palindrome! And there's a berry bush right over there!" He sidled up to it calmly but picked up speed when he saw a fat raccoon heading in the same direction at the same speed. By the time they got to the bush, both were panting and out of breath after running as fast as they could in an effort to beat the other.

Both picked as many berries as they could carry and ran off, oddly, both in the direction of Niko and

Cawyer's camp. Niko wondered why until the raccoon gave a sudden burst of speed and rammed Niko in the legs. He fell and dropped all his berries. The raccoon chuckled to himself, scooped up the berries in his arms, and ran off. "Little pest!" Niko shouted. He ran after the ring-tailed rascal.

"Little pest! shouted Cawyer. He ran at full speed after the fox that had taken the stick. Since squids aren't made for running around on dry land, and having legs doesn't necessarily mean you're a strong runner, Cawyer quickly fell behind. After a fit of panting and wheezing, he looked up and said, "Maybe I should get an inhaler."

He took in his surroundings. "Where am I?" He was lost. The entire forest was unfamiliar. Then he jerked his head to one direction. He saw something. A man-like shape was visibly rambling around in the sunlight, casting an obvious shadow. "Bigfoot!" exclaimed Cawyer. He ran off in the figure's direction.

Niko ran off in the raccoon's direction. When he came to an intersection in the woods, he stopped for a sort of traffic light comprised of fireflies. Tons of animals ran by in a big rush before Niko could go. "Are those synapsids?"

When the traffic passed, Niko ran off after the raccoon again. He soon made it to a tree with a hollow the raccoon had squeezed into. He peered inside. "I know you're in there!" he shouted.

The raccoon clambered into a room inside the tree. He walked up to a red squirrel sitting at a game table in the center of the room. He laid the red berries in the middle of the table. The squirrel laid some blue-berries down. Then they dealt cards the size of pins and played poker for the berries.

Niko finally fit his head into the hollow of the tree and looked down upon the scene. "Found you!" he exclaimed.

The raccoon scooped up all the berries on the table and ran through a back door in the tree. The squirrel chittered loudly and angrily and shook his fist at the raccoon for stealing all the berries. "I know, I'm mad at him too," said Niko.

Niko pulled his head out of the tree and looked beyond it. The raccoon was running away as fast as it could. Niko ran as fast as his legs would carry him. However, his legs were a bit feisty today. Here's what happened to him in the next six seconds in a nutshell:

His legs slipped, his feet tripped, birds flew in his face, a snake hissed at his toes, a red panda laughed at him, a mockingbird mocked him, a hummingbird hummed to him, a whip-poor-will whipped him, and a Gila monster bit him. Now, all that the animals had to do was to push the raccoon up to him.

The raccoon stared at him.

Hard.

Niko held up his forefinger matter-of-factly, opened his mouth to say something, and fell to the ground unconscious. The animals all cheered and began to pickpocket him, delighted at how much they'd managed to collect from a bumbling old fool in dopey gloves.

Meanwhile, Cawyer was still groping through the woods, searching for the bigfoot-like figure he saw earlier. He saw movement again. This time it came in the form of rustling bushes. "Ah-ha!" shouted Cawyer. He leaped for the bushes, ready to dominate them. Suddenly the bushes opened up for some reason.

"YAH!" shouted Cawyer. He went over the edge of a cliff, but quickly grasped on to the wall of the cliff with his suckers. "Help! Help!" he shouted. He looked around. There was no branch or rock jutting out he could put pressure on to climb back up. He decided to try climbing up using his suckers.

Before he could even begin, he saw the fox, of course, with a little wood duck friend. There they were standing up there, in safety, peering down to see Cawyer gripping for his life. They made a sound that seemed to be laughing at him. "I would ask help from you," he called up, "if you weren't so indescribably evil. Come to gloat? I think you've already started."

The fox grabbed the stick it had stolen from Cawyer at the camp from its mouth with its hand. He pointed it down the cliff, holding it down to Cawyer's hand.

"Are you going to help me back up, fox?" asked Cawyer to the fox. "Is this for real?"

It wasn't. The fox used the stick to simply pry Cawyer's hand from the wall of the cliff.

"Stop!" shouted Cawyer. He screamed.

He fell.

CHAPTER 7

Falling is a sensation in which taste, sight, hearing, and smell are paralyzed. All that remains is the feeling of every organ in your body floating to the top because of the force and the wind whooshing by.

After about three seconds, Cawyer fell to the ground. He took so long because he had to fall through a large canopy of trees. After he gathered his strength, he stood up and looked around. The rustling was heard again. "Where are you?" he called out. He saw the figure again, closer this time, and he ran up to it. He saw faint hints of fur all over its body. "Bigfoot, surely," he said.

He leaped for the figure. It turned around suddenly. Cawyer could see an ape-like face and wrinkled, gray hands carrying an instant camera, which flashed in Cawyer's face. Cawyer screamed a Tarzan cry and landed on the ground in front of the gorilla guy.

He lunged for it and squirted ink in its face the moment it took another picture. Then it disappeared.

"Darn it," said Cawyer. "My instinct mechanism backfired. I created the diversion he needed to escape.

He climbed up the cliffside using his suckers. When he got to the top, his gaze fell upon the fox that had stolen the stick from him. It was holding the stick in its mouth. "Now you're toast!" he told the fox, then chased after him, though it wasn't easy. "I hate having eyes on either side of my head." he said. "It gives you zero depth perception!"

It wasn't easy, but Cawyer finally got the stick from the fox. He returned to the camp the same time Niko did. Cawyer looked at the leaves and twigs in Niko's hair, the hole in the knee of his pants, and his two bare feet, one red and the other purple. Niko looked at the ink-stained Cawyer (he had no bruises from his fall because squid skin heals quickly).

"What happened to you?" they asked each other in unison.

Niko and Cawyer gazed at each other in pure astonishment, almost unable to believe what had happened to the other person. "I'll explain it later," they told each other.

Cawyer started the fire. Niko set out the small rabble of berries he had collected. Then the two roasted berries over the fire.

"How'd collecting berries go?" Cawyer asked Niko.

"Fine," Niko replied. "Have any trouble collecting sticks for the fire?"

"Nah. I did meet Bigfoot though."

"Bigfoot?"

"Yeah. Some weird ape-looking guy with a man-like stance. Well, he actually didn't have big feet, and he wasn't that tall, so he was more like a sasquatch." After some silence he added, "I'm sorry our quest to get you the money you need to pay rent isn't as easy as I said it would be."

"It's fine. My second day has ended, and I only have one day left to pay rent, but it's fine."

"I remember once living in an apartment as a kid. Every day we'd order take-out from this cool fast-food place I can't remember the name of. We lived next-door to this grumpy porcupinefish family that hated balloons."

"Speak of the devil…"

"Say what?"

Niko pointed into the blackness of the forest. There, hanging just outside the bright light of the flame, was a small, frowning porcupinefish.

It crawled up next to them on all fours and whispered in a small, husky voice that gave them pictures of death in their minds, "The ##### ##### that has stolen your ### has sent me to #### you."

"Why do you keep bleeping out your words?" asked Cawyer.

"So I can say whatever I want without giving information of my master's plans to you." He adopted a warlike stance, his spines aiming for the two friends.

"You work for the tiger shark that stole our gem, don't you? You've been sent to kill us, haven't you?" asked Niko.

"Darn it, how'd you know it was me?"

"That's how we roll!" said Cawyer. "Come on, Niko! We can take him!"

"Uh… Cawyer?"

"Whoopee!" Cawyer leaped from the log he was sitting on and landed upon the porcupinefish. The creature seemed to flatten under Cawyer. "I knew it!" said Cawyer. "We can take this wimp!" Suddenly, he let out a scream of pain. "YEEOW!" Cawyer hopped from the spot and landed a few yards away.

The porcupinefish had inflated to full size. All his quills were pointing out straight. "The name is Sharpfin," it said. "And neither of you will make it out of here alive." He deflated to his original size and magically produced a blow gun from behind his body. He plucked a quill from his back and shot it.

"Whoa!" The quill headed straight for Cawyer. The shot fired true, though the quill ended up behind Cawyer.

"What? How?" asked Sharpfin.

Cawyer smiled. "I have no bones. I'm just skin, flesh, and organs!"

Sharpfin decided Cawyer was a lost cause, so he aimed for Niko and shot. Niko flinched and held his arms out instinctively... and the quill never hit him! Niko opened his eyes and watched the quill. He was holding it in the air with his futuristic gloves.

"How?" asked Sharpfin in utter disbelief.

Niko grinned. "These things just seem to happen." He twisted it around and pushed straight back toward Sharpfin.

Sharpfin gulped.

The quill landed straight between the eyes. "Yes! Right between the eyes! Just like David and Goliath!" Niko cheered.

Sharpfin scoffed. "Unfortunately for you, I'm not Goliath." He plucked the quill from his forehead and shot it at Niko. He stopped it and sent it back to him. Sharpfin once again tried to impale Cawyer. Cawyer's

buoyant body remained resilient. He began to shoot
Niko and Cawyer in turn. He couldn't get a shot in.

"How. Is. This. Possible?!" he shouted in frustration. Once he was almost out of quills, he inflated
himself into a giant ball and began to roll toward them
like a bowling ball or a stray cannonball.

"Help!" screamed Niko. He hopped onto a log to
avoid the rolling menace. Cawyer did, too. Sharpfin
rolled on top of the fire and put it out. "That was good,
considering we didn't have to put it out ourselves."

Sharpfin rolled after one of the logs, the log that
Niko was standing on, and bumped it. "Argh!" said
Niko as it began to roll away from the camp. He posi-
tioned himself in a worthy stance and began to walk
back toward the camp. He found this caused him to
roll farther away, so he began to stumble backwards,
and the log rolled toward the sentient sphere.

Sharpfin rolled toward Cawyer and bumped him,
causing his log to roll as well. He attempted to walk
backwards, copying Niko, but his tentacles simply
stuck to the log, and he rolled with it, his body splayed
across the entire surface area of the log like a slipcover.
He crashed somewhere in the infinite dark forest.

"Cawyer!" called Niko.

CHAPTER 8

Niko tried to run towards Cawyer, but that just made the log roll backwards. "Oops. Forgot!" He pushed off the log, letting it roll at great speed in the opposite direction, and ran towards Cawyer.

The log, however, kept rolling. It ricocheted off of a tree and rolled toward Sharpfin. Sharpfin screamed and found himself flattened and deflated by it.

With rekindled anger, the porcupinefish reinflated and rolled toward the two buddies. Flattening peonies, cornflowers, and dandelions, he was determined to kill them and anything that got in his way.

"Are you okay?" asked Niko, helping Cawyer up from the ground on which he had fell, knotted with the log he had rolled with.

"I've had better days," Cawyer groaned, feeling horrible because there was no spine to stretch and straighten.

He hopped onto the log he was rolling before. He snatched two large leaves from the ground and used his suckers to stick them onto his feet. This would prevent his suckers from plastering his feet to the unstable log, thus causing the log to bring him down with it.

Niko hopped onto his log and, after some careful balancing, found his key, though precariously poised, position. Then he and Cawyer rolled around to get their balance.

Niko rolled toward camp immediately. However, Cawyer chose to simply roll around in a circle. He attempted an ollie, though met disappointment.

"C'mon, Cawyer!" said Niko. "We've got a job to do!"

"I'm coming, I'm coming."

Sharpfin screamed. The two rolled toward him from different directions and smushed him between them, deflating him.

"Ooh...," said Niko.

"That's got to hurt," said Cawyer.

There, on the ground, lay the sad, insignificant-looking form of Sharpfin, now resembling a popped balloon. He brought his face upwards, a bruised, battered, noseless monstrosity. He scowled at Niko and Cawyer.

"Sorry," said Cawyer. "But you were trying to kill us, so..."

"You boys have made a grave error."

"How so?"

"I will be back! I will be back! I will be back stronger and better and smarter and bigger! I will be back! I will beEEEEOW!" That last, strangled cry sounded the arrival of Niko's sneaker coming down and crushing the once-mercenary.

"That's the end of him," said Niko. They walked off and left the puddle of nothing to himself.

"You know, I really wish we had known we were going to have an epic quest like this and a 50\50 chance of finding that crystal," said Cawyer. "Then we could have brought our bicycles.

"Oh, don't remind me. I'm not a big fan of long-distance hikes. The farthest I've ever had to walk was from one end of the south half of the South Carolina coast to the other, on a family trip."

"That's rough."

The two of them were so busy talking that they didn't notice Sharpfin was inching away from the spot he was before. "Those dopes," he whispered to himself. "They wouldn't notice a blue whale playing basketball in a pigpen."

He crawled up to the bike pump they had been lugging along with them and used it to reinflate himself. "Ah, that's much better," he said. He rolled up to the buddies, who were using giant leaves to create comfortable spots to sleep for the night.

"Goodnight, Niko," said Cawyer.

"Goodnight, CawAAAAH!" Niko exclaimed as he was suddenly yanked away from his bed.

"What the—" said Cawyer. With his night vision abilities, he could see perfectly what was happening. Niko, on the other hand...

"What's happening?!"

"It looks like Sharpfin is back from the dead, and he's strangling you."

"Uh-huh!" said Sharpfin. He threw Niko on top of Cawyer.

Cawyer screamed. "Whoa!" he shouted. He held out his arms. Niko landed in them, and then fell safely to the floor.

"Whew!" said Niko. "Are you okay?"

Cawyer shrugged. "More or less."

Niko gasped. "Did you break your arms?"

"Nah. I don't have any bones to break in the first place! They've just gone limp for a minute."

"Phew!"

"Besides, it's just two arms."

"You're right. Two arms aren't much of a loss."

"Hey!" shouted Sharpfin.

They both jerked their heads toward him.

"Eyes on the porcupinefish. I may not be strong enough to fight you tonight, and I may have lost most my confidence, but I can't leave you without a little 'goodbye' gift!" Sharpfin began to pluck quills from his back. He took everyone he had left, though some had grown back rapidly. He began to piece them together like a 3-D puzzle. Niko and Cawyer looked at each other, then back at Sharpfin.

Sharpfin slipped the last quill into place. He grinned and held up his masterpiece in the air. Niko's and Cawyer's eyes widened. Sharpfin had created a sort of axe, the blade made up of the sharp ends of the quills.

"What are you going to do with that?" asked Cawyer.

"Say goodbye to each other!" He chopped the nearest tree down. It began to fall towards them. "Au revoir!" He scurried off.

Niko screamed. The tree fell on top of Cawyer.

The moment the tree hit the original site of the campfire, it ignited. It wasn't very big, and didn't set anything else on fire, so Niko let it burn. "Cawyer!" he called out.

"Niko?" asked a weak voice.

"Cawyer! Don't worry, buddy, I'm coming for you!"

Niko ran to the other side of the tree. "Cawyer! Where are you?!"

"Under here!" Niko ran to where he heard the voice. He saw Cawyer struggling to get out from under the burning tree. "Cawyer!" Niko grabbed hold of the limp arms and tried to pull Cawyer out from under the tree.

His arms came free without resistance.

"AAAAAAAAAAAGGGHHH!

Cawyer chuckled. "Don't scream, Niko. Happens all the time. They'll grow back."

Niko sighed with relief. He grabbed two more of Cawyer's arms and tugged him out. "I'm sorry for not using my special gloves quick enough to save you, Cawyer."

"Hey, it's not your fault. You just didn't have quick enough reflexes. I can totally relate!"

Niko smiled at his friend. Though he had just been crushed by a burning tree, Cawyer was virtually alright. His skin would have healed from any bruises or splinters by now, and his oily, constantly moist skin would have temporarily protected him from fire damage.

"Well, shall we eat now?"

"Totally."

CHAPTER 9

Niko pulled up the logs he and Cawyer were sitting on. Cawyer gathered the berries. Then they began to roast berries over the fire for supper once again.

"Want to hear a scary story?" asked Niko.

"Eh. What's it about?"

"It's about a wicked witch who summons an army of dragons that band together to destroy the kingdom of—"

"Sounds like a fantasy novel."

Niko sighed. "You're right."

Some silence…

The clouds covered up the moon, giving them limited light.

"How much longer do you think it will take?" asked Cawyer.

"What?" asked Niko.

"The journey."

"If we walk nonstop all day, my guess is we'll be there by noon tomorrow. Then we swoop into that mean old shark's base, get the crystal back, and go home. If Sharpfin was that shark's only mercenary, and we have to assume he might return like he said, then we might just pull it off and return before sunset. That's when Percy will evict me."

"Great."

They packed up the berries and shoved the sticks away. They put out the fire by smothering it with leaves. Then they lay in their beds.

"Goodnight, Cawyer," said Niko.

"Goodnight, Niko," said Cawyer.

They dozed off.

Then they heard something.

• • •

Sharpfin scurried into a small hole in the ground, just big enough to fit his deflated form. He then scurried through a long, straight tunnel to his goal: the shark's castle. He had used this same tunnel to get from the castle to the two friends.

He worked for the evil tiger shark.

Sharpfin ran in front of the castle. He waited patiently for the drawbridge to be lowered and ran across it inside the castle when it was. The castle was made of a dark brick and had a moat of lava that cast a mile-long light and heat waves in every direction.

Sharpfin sweated as he stumbled inside and winked at the guards in gorilla suits that guarded every inch of the fortress. Not just because of the perspiration from the heat of the molten liquid below, though that was about ninety-seven percent of the reason. He was also very stressed. He was worried that he would be punished for not successfully exterminating the two buddies who would mess with his employer's plans.

He walked through the giant halls that populated the castle, carrying great paintings from famous painters and beautiful antique vases on small three-legged tables. He came to a large parking lot with many cars and trucks that the shark had acquired from his other ventures.

There was nearly every model imaginable, all the way from 1941. If you came here, you might think it was rather strange to find all these cars here, with no order to sort them by and no way to drive them out of the parking lot. It could be a sort of maze, a last-chance defense mechanism against those who had never been here.

He bowed respectfully to every guard he saw and soon came to the throne room. He took a deep, nervous breath, swung the doors open, and stepped inside.

"Hello, Cheef," he said to the giant shark sitting in the throne.

Cheef twirled his staff like a baton and looked at the porcupinefish. "Hello, Sharpfin. Has your mission been successful?"

"W-well, sir, uh, I kind of, sort of…," he winced, "was defeated by them."

Cheef looked pointedly at Sharpfin. "I'm sorry, what was that?

Come on, tell me. Don't stall."

Sharpfin gulped. "I maybe, might of, kind of, accidentally, inadvertently…been defeated and chased away."

"WHAT?!" Cheef slammed his staff down on the armrest of his throne. "What did I tell you? 'Find them and kill them!' Is that so much to ask?! And stop using multiple commas in every sentence! It's very annoying!"

"N-no. But I did say I would retur—"

"You have failed me, Sharpfin! You know how angry and frustrated I can get when one fails me, is that right, Sharpfin?!"

"Uh, yes."

"How do you plead?"

"I was planning to return! I told them I would be back stronger and bigger and smarter and better! All I need, all I'm asking for is a little help! Maybe from some of your guards, or—"

"Help, Sharpfin? You told me you could do it! You told me you could do it all by yourself and that you didn't need any help from anyone!"

"Well, yeah, sir, but—"

"But?! BUT?! But what?! What else do you need to accomplish this task that I have given you that you said you could accomplish?!"

"Uh—"

"And don't use dashes at the end of every sentence!"

"That wouldn't happen if you wouldn't keep interrupting me!"

"You do know what the penalty for failing at one of my demands is, right?"

Sharpfin didn't speak. He was sweating enough to be an ice cream cone on a hot summer's afternoon."

"I SAID 'YOU DO KNOW WHAT THE PENALTY FOR FAILING AT ONE OF MY DEMANDS IS, RIGHT?!'"

Sharpfin nearly fainted. "Yes," he squeaked.

"Kill him!" Cheef pointed his staff at Sharpfin.

"NO! Please!" shouted Sharpfin, beginning to shed tears, though it was impossible to tell his tears from his sweat. Two guards ran up and strangled Sharpfin by the arms. Sharpfin tried to fight his way out of it, though he was very ineffective without many of his quills. He was dragged through the exit and led to the moat, where he would be thrown in.

The simplest form of execution.

Cheef threw his staff down in frustration. He groaned and rubbed his temples. Nothing was working. He had to kill them. No matter if they continued on with their journey or returned to society, he'd be in big trouble.

Cheef jerked his head up. "Spy!" he called out.

A person in a gorilla suit hurried into the room.

"How is your expert spying going on? Have you made any new advances?"

The spy nodded and gave Cheef some Polaroids. Cheef flipped through them. Earlier ones revealing evidence of Niko and Cawyer's quest to retake ownership of the crystal he flipped through immediately. They were of no interest to him. They were the only reason he knew about Niko and Cawyer's quest.

CHAPTER 10

Cheef soon came to the newest, most recent photos. There were three. A snapshot of Niko and Cawyer departing from each other at camp, a snapshot of Cawyer lunging towards the spy, and a completely black photo.

"Has this photo not developed yet?" asked Cheef.

The spy grunted and shook his head.

"You say the squid shot ink into the camera?"

The spy nodded. He held up the stained camera. That was the last photo he took. The Polaroid camera was no longer reliable, much less useful.

"Very well. When this little conference of ours is finished, please report to our technology room. They will give you a new camera and some extra Polaroids. Understood?"

The spy nodded.

"Anything else? Perhaps the reason this squid found you and was attacking you?"

The spy grunted and walked around in a small circle, holding his arms out like a zombie and growling. He was also making emphasized stomping motions with his hairy feet.

"You say he thought you were Bigfoot?!"

The spy stopped and nodded. He held out Cheef's staff to him.

Cheef took it. He threw his head back in wild guffaws. "Of course! Excellent thinking! The perfect cover!

That stupid squid has inadvertently provided us with a reason for an ape-like figure roaming around in the woods! Keep up the good work! And remain elusive!"

The spy nodded. He walked off toward the technology room with the ink-stained camera.

Cheef groaned. "I knew sending out a super small guy like Sharpfin wouldn't work. He's not smart enough or strong enough. Now they probably know I'm on to them." He glared at nothing in particular and said, "Check that; they definitely know I'm on to them! Well, they won't get away with it forever! I know another assassin that is better than Sharpfin and will fight to the death!"

He threw his head back and called as loud as he could, "CODE NAME: TIGERSTRIPES!"

A sea turtle rushed into the room. She rushed in suddenly and right away, as if she had been there the entire time. She was wearing an eyepatch and a bandana around her leg. "You rang?"

"I have a very important task for you. There are two, er, problems, effective to my grand plan, that are inching closer and closer towards my castle. They go by the names of Niko and Cawyer."

"What would you like me to do with them?"

"You are a mercenary, right?"

"Yes."

He leaned in close. "Are you sure you are feeling up to the task?"

The sea turtle straightened up. "I will serve you faithfully in any battle, and on any quest you send me on. I will not quit until I or the other side dies first. They will not escape, lest I am deceased."

"Find them. And kill them!"

• • •

Silence…

"What was that sound?!" whispered Niko, afraid in the dark.

"I have no idea," said Cawyer, who was used to the dark and had lived in it nearly his entire life.

It began to rain from the cloudy sky. It put out the campfire.

"It is me," said a scholarly, matter-of-fact voice.

"What?" Niko ignited a stick. He held it up to the person, though the rain extinguished it instantly. A bolt of lightning illuminated the person, revealing him to be a chartreuse catfish.

"Allow me to introduce myself," said the catfish. He was wearing glasses supported by his mustache and carried a brown briefcase. "My name is Whiskers Wayne. I represent a company that sells things like vacuum cleaners and fluorescent lightbulbs, but right now I'm selling stock!"

"Selling stock?"

"Yeah! Imagine! Putting $5–$29 in and receiving $100–$754 back!"

"I can imagine it. I can't imagine actually doing it."

"Why not?"

"Why can't you just leave us alone?"

"Why in the world? Buying stock can be really effective."

"Yeah, to the solicitors who sell it," muttered Cawyer, laughing under his breath.

"Didn't you see our floor mat that says, No Solicitors?"

"No."

"Darn it, Cawyer, we forgot to put down a No Solicitors floor mat!"

"We are failures," Cawyer said sarcastically, rolling his eyes.

"Look, boys," said Whiskers. "I believe you will be most pleased by my sto—"

"Buzz off!" shouted Niko, waving his arms at him to shoo him away.

"See ya, short stuff," said Cawyer. The two walked off.

Whiskers grumbled in frustration and gathered his things.

"Boy that guy sure is a drag, eh, Cawyer?"

"Yeah. Not very biblical."

"What does that mean?"

"Not very nice."

Niko made a face of sarcasm. "Yeah, but 'biblical' generally means 'Hark!' and 'the cedars of Lebanon!' and 'do unto others as you would have them do unto you!', right?"

"Eh."

"Eh?! EH?! That's what you say?! It took me two years of bible therapy to get the knowledge of the Bible needed to entail my wisdom unto you!"

"You must have been fidgety and inattentive in church," Cawyer muttered under his breath, giggling.

"Hey, no wise cracks!"

They glared at each other for a minute, though only Cawyer could actually see what was happening. Niko squared his shoulders. Cawyer would have too if he had had shoulders.

Cawyer yawned. "Can we just get on with our duties? We've been up all night debating the Bible! "I'll bet a quarter we won't wake up until 11:00 tomorrow morning! We had planned an 8:00 a.m. wake-up, didn't we?"

Niko nodded. He shrugged and softened his shoulders. "You're right. 8:00 a.m., on the button."

"Shall we?"

"You first."

"Thank you!"

They each nuzzled in close with their leaf mattresses.

"Goodnight, Niko."

"Goodnight, Cawyer."

They dozed off…

"Seriously, boys—"

"AAGH!"

CHAPTER 11

"All right pal, you got to go!" Niko picked up Whiskers and put him down farther away from the camp.

"Oh, come on!" pleaded Whiskers. "It's so fun!"

"To buy stock? You've got to be kidding!"

"But—"

"No! No means no! This has gone on for too long! We don't want to buy stock, and you know that. So why won't you just shut up and leave us alone?!"

"Because I cannot fail!" he declared, holding his fin high in the air for emphasis. "You are my first customers for over twenty-three years!"

Cawyer scoffed. "I couldn't possibly imagine why."

"Look pal, we want nothing more of you, your stock, and your lame briefcase!"

Whiskers gasped. "My briefcase is cool, I thought!"

"Are you kidding? It looks like a swarm of grasshoppers ran over it!"

Whiskers peered behind Niko. "Is he always this imaginative with his insults?" he asked Cawyer.

"Hey, I'm right here!" exclaimed Niko.

Cawyer shrugged. "Not ordinarily."

"Less vague, please."

Suddenly, he was chucked off the sheer rock cliff face that Niko had to scale earlier that day. The action was committed by none other than Niko himself, who had had quite enough of the annoying man for some time.

"Niko!" exclaimed Cawyer. "How could you do such a thing?!"

Niko flexed his muscles. "A strong arm and a hate for salespeople. A newfound hate, actually."

"Niko! You might even be worse than the tiger shark we're after!"

"Oh, please. Cawyer. He stole a jewel!"

"And you chucked someone over the side of a cliff, where they may be imminently falling to their doom, or worse, already dead!"

Niko groaned. "Let's just get some sleep. We stay on one subject for too long, we become one of the unlucky ones who doesn't get what they want. "Can you believe how boring a buddy movie like that might be?"

"Uh…"

Picture it! Two buddies, entrusting each other, until the night they forget to fall asleep and are doomed to a late fate!"

Niko, you're staying on one subject for too long. If you continue this, what you have predicted may come true."

"How do you know?"

Cawyer held up a stopwatch and smiled. "I always know. I'm the master of time."

"Cawyer! Where did you get that?"

"Lucky for me, scholarly people like Whiskers always have stopwatches hanging outside of their briefcases. I remember the giant stopwatch the White Rabbit had in *Alice in Wonderland*. I always thought he kept it hanging out because it simply would not fit inside. But now I guess it's a trend among those people. Anyway, I saw it hanging out, and when you picked him up to throw him off the cliff, I grabbed it, and when you threw him off, causing Whiskers and his briefcase to pull away from me, my super strong suckers did the rest!"

"Wow," said Niko, placing his hands on his temples. The recent events were very much to process.

"Um… Shall we sleep now?" asked Cawyer.

"Oh, yeah!" said Niko, coming out of his daydream. He rested in his leafy bed. It wasn't too uncomfortable, though the night was very chilly, and his teeth chattered.

Cawyer, who was used to such cold temperatures, being a squid and all, did not have chattering teeth. That may have been because he did not have any teeth. But a chattering beak is not all that comfortable either.

"Goodnight, Cawyer," said Niko, urging himself to rest.

"Goodnight, Niko," said Cawyer.

The two buddies finally dozed off for the night. Their gentle Zs could be heard by the nocturnal creatures.

• • •

Soon, they woke up. "Good morning, Cawyer," said Niko, stretching.

"Good morning, Niko," said Cawyer. Unlike Niko, his rubbery body permitted him the ability to not need to stretch.

"What's the plan for today?"

"Oh, just wait until you hear my epic battle plan!" He pulled out the stopwatch. "It's 10:00. Perfect! Your rent is due at 4:50. We'll walk nonstop until the tiger shark's base is in view. Then we have a rest, eat some berries, and march inside. Then one of us neutralizes and distracts the shark, the other locates and picks up the crystal, and we both go home."

"Excellent! If we leave now, we should have some time to spare before my deadline."

"No time to waste then!"

The two packed up all they had, carrying it in their arms, and walked off towards the end of the forest. "I think we'll be leaving this place for another biome by now," said Cawyer.

"That's too bad," remarked Niko. I kind of like it." He gestured to the amazingly beautiful environment around them. The colorful trees were accompanied by rhododendrons, pea shoots, grapevines, fallen apples, rabbits, and blue jays. It wasn't all rainbows and lollipops and baseball bats, however. A snake was making a scrawny snack out of a slow squirrel. Two rhinoceros beetles were wrestling.

Cawyer scoffed. "Good riddance, I say. The wild plants stick to my suckers, and I'm covered with bug bites and scratches."

"Wrong. *I'm* covered in bug bites and scratches. That's quite the opposite. You couldn't be covered in bug bites and scratches if you tried."

"Well, you've got a point there." He paused. "But I would be!"

"We've quite a journey ahead of us."

"Quite, quite true, my friend."

They marched onwards. Soon, they came to the edge of the tree line. They stood on the edge of the infamous cliff. They looked down upon a wild field of tall, swaying grasses. Potato beetles and rats crawled among them.

"It's quite nice," remarked Cawyer. "At least in comparison to that forest."

"Oh, please. You can't possibly prefer this."

"It's peaceful."

"It's sparse. And colorless."

"You can't be picky."

"I guess we must have creative differences."

Yeah."

Suddenly, someone pushed them off the side of the cliff.

CHAPTER 12

Ah, falling.

I know we discussed it earlier in this story, but I do have more to say.

Falling is a feeling you may have experienced in dreams (most likely) or in reality. I once had a particular exhilarating dream in which I swung upon a rope above a lily pad-infested bog. The falling sensation was strong there. Falling feels like you are a box with a soft, fragile surface, like a cardboard box. As you might know, smaller, lighter objects fall much slower than larger, heavier objects. Likewise, objects in a box will "fall" upwards inside the box as it falls downwards, and that is how it feels to fall. You are the box, and it feels like all your organs and bones are the objects inside. It almost feels like everything in your body is trying to pull you back up, which might just be what the heck is happening. That actually makes a lot of sense. Additionally, liquid inside a storage unit will float upwards when the storage unit is falling downwards, giving you the feeling that you're turning into a liquid as you fall, and objects inside a box will fall downwards if the box is being pulled upwards by some indescribable force at a great speed.

As you may have guessed, I can go on and on about the wonders of falling for pages, but that's not what this chapter, let alone this book, is really about. So I'll stop this and move on to the story again.

Niko and Cawyer fell and fell and fell. It didn't seem like they would ever stop.

Niko looked up, hoping to get a glance of the horrible person who had pushed them. He didn't see anything. This next assassin must have been quick.

Niko didn't want to mess with him. But what else could it be? Who else hated them enough to push them off the side of a cliff? Niko could only think of three possibilities: 1) A new assassin, 2) The tiger shark himself, and 3) Whiskers Wayne. After all, he had thrown the guy off a cliff. Unless Whiskers really was one of the assassins and had merely disguised himself as a salesperson to get close to them and gain their trust.

Well, he didn't.

Niko watched Cawyer. Cawyer, unused to falling (at least until recently), was struggling to keep hold of consciousness. Eventually, he gave in.

Niko averted his attention downwards. He saw the small cluster of trees they were about to fall into. He didn't know how they could survive the fall.

Unless...

It was a desperate choice, but what did they have to lose?

Your lives, Niko thought.

"Shut up," said Niko.

He spread one arm towards the ground and one towards Cawyer. He had to save Cawyer. The guy could take a lot, but if he hit the forest floor, he would be squashed into calamari. The psychic energy of his gloves began to ripple out in waves. Suddenly, there was resistance, and Niko was held in the air just cen-timeters from the ground. He took a few deep breaths and glanced up at Cawyer, who was hanging helplessly in midair.

"Phew," said Niko.

After a few seconds, he let go.

The two dropped to the floor. Cawyer woke up and wheezed. "Are we dead?"

"No."

"That's a relief."

"No, not really," said a new voice. They looked up. "It means I now have to pummel you with my wrath. I really thought the fall would finish you and my job would be done easy. But this one here," she pointed to Niko, "is very innovative."

"I'm sorry," said Cawyer, "who are you?"

The sea turtle peered down at them. She wore a utility belt, black bandana, and eyepatch. The bandana was wrapped around her leg. "My name is Tigerstripes. And I'm the greatest assassin since sliced bread!"

There was a pause…

"Sliced bread was an assassin?" asked Cawyer, look-ing at Niko.

"Whatever you plan on doing, we can take it!" said Niko. "Nothing can surprise us anymore!"

"We've seen the toughest of the toughest! The sharpest of the sharpest!"

"The annoying-est of the annoying-est!"

"Yes, but you've probably never seen my version of sharp! As you know, sharp has two meanings. Cunning and pointy." She rocked on the balls of her feet, pulled two knives out of her utility belt, and grinned. "And I have both."

She began to hurl knives at them from her seemingly bottomless utility belt.

"Cawyer, get down!" shouted Niko, who hit the dirt. He did try to deflect the knives and even shoot them back at her using his gloves.

Cawyer, who was completely defenseless, had only one option: to curl up in a ball and hope the knives went right through or glanced harmlessly off of his rubbery flesh.

"How are you two so defiant? So hard to defeat? All Cheef said was you were two goofballs threatening to his plan."

"Goofballs?!"

"Yeah! And that you were silly!"

"SILLY?!?!?!"

"AARRRRRGHHGGGGGGG!"

"Ooh!" said Cawyer. That'd be a nice outburst of anger to hang on my mantel."

"You shall never survive!" shouted Tigerstripes. She hurled more knives at them.

"Want to bet?" Niko hopped in the air and attempted to redirect all the knives with his powers.

But there were too many.

Butcher knives, butter knives, bread knives, four-star restaurant kitchen knives, five-star restaurant kitchen knives, average restaurant kitchen knives, penknives, hand knives, sporks, oyster-shucking knives, onion-skinning knives, and coconut-shucking knives.

"Where did you get all these knives?!" shouted Cawyer.

"Skill, perseverance, materials, and a fiery forge!"

"Can you just hold down on the knives for a small while? We need some time to regroup," asked Niko.

"And why exactly should I do that?" She paused throwing knives.

"Um… well…"

"That's right! You have no reason."

Niko sighed. "I guess you're right there."

"Of course! I knew it. I always am. Now step aside!" Tigerstripes pulled out a shotgun and loaded it with knives.

"What are you going to do with that?" asked Cawyer.

"Cawyer!" shouted Niko. "Don't let your guard down!"

"I'm going to kill you!" Tigerstripes shouted. "Now, please stay in one spot you two. If my calculations are correct, and there may be no reason to say 'if' because they almost always are, this will end in bloodshed!"

Tigerstripes hurled an insane barrage of knives at them.

CHAPTER 13

"No!" screamed Cawyer, and he closed his eyes tight as he could…

…but he didn't need to. "Niko?"

Niko was using his gloves to block the knives. They had assaulted them from every direction. Butcher knives, butter knives, bread knives… well, you get the picture. Lots of knives. Anyway, Niko had twisted his body in every which way he could and had extended his power as wide as he could, to accomplish such a feat.

"Darnity darnity darn darn darny darn!" shouted Tigerstripes, stomping her foot in anger. "I must not fail! Tigerstripes will achieve! You'll see! Ha ha!" She twisted an ordinary kitchen knife around so that it faced her (who knows what she was planning?), then yelped as Niko moved his finger just so, and the knife went straight for her eye. She stumbled back in pain, removed the knife, then moved her eyepatch to the injured eye, revealing a perfect eye underneath. She later remarked, "I was saving it!"

"Niko! You saved us!" said Cawyer in glee.

"I did, eh?" He grunted with the strain of the task. "Now, I'm going to let these knives go soon. They've lost momentum already. They should simply drop to the ground. It's not like I hit the 'pause' button on a TV remote. Now, Cawyer—" He eyed Cawyer, and gasped. "Cawyer!"

"What" asked Cawyer. He was twirling a knife about eye level with him with the tip of his arm. It was a simple bread knife with serrated edges.

"Don't do that! I can't hold on to these knives forever! If something were to go wrong when I dropped these, you could die!"

"Oh, please, Niko. I'm a very stable creature! What are the chances of that?"

"Says the guy who has no bones and lets blowdarts and knives shot at him somehow end up on a surface on the other side of his body!"

"Well, okay, you've got airtight logic there. But what could possibly go wrong?!"

"Every time anyone ever says that, something goes wrong."

"Oops! Do you think I jinxed it or something?"

Niko sighed. "Just don't touch any knives!"

"Don't worry! This squid ain't going to touch nothing!" He attempted to lean on something like cool dudes do when they're chill and relaxed, but, leaning and not touching anything, he leaned farther and farther until he tripped and the tip of his arm caught on the bread knife, which essentially impaled it. "Oops."

Niko glanced in his direction, then sighed. "Well, you were right about one thing."

"What's that?"

He looked at him darkly. "About you not touching nothing."

The sea turtle, peering through the window of knives, giggled with glee at their current predicament.

"You dummies aren't going to get out of there alive!" she shouted in.

"Oh yeah?!" shouted Cawyer. "Well, we'll just have to see about that, why don't we?!" He turned to Niko. "What do we do, friend?"

Niko sighed again. "I don't think we *are* going to get out of this mess, Cawyer."

Cawyer's sad eyes blinked at Niko. "You don't have a plan?"

"No, I don't."

Cawyer looked down. "Is there any hope at all?"

"No, I don't think so. I'm losing not only hope in getting out of here, but also losing strength in holding these knives up."

"No! Hold on just a few more seconds, Niko!" Cawyer tugged at his arm, trying to get the knife out of it.

"Goodbye, Cawyer," said Niko, tears in his eyes. He let go of the knives.

"NOOOOOOOOOOOOOOO!!" shouted Cawyer.

"YEEEEEEEEEAAAAAAAH!!" shouted Tigerstripes. She produced a boombox from out of nowhere and some sunglasses and began to dance to the boombox's funky bass riffs.

All the knives fell to the ground. The knife that had held Cawyer's arm in place fell to the ground, taking Cawyer's arm with it, but otherwise he remained unharmed.

Tigerstripes heard the knives clatter to the ground with a crashing sound she had never before heard, and it drowned out the boombox's funky tunes. She peered over the edge of the hill she had been standing on the entire time and whispered, "What happens next?"

Niko looked at Cawyer. Cawyer looked at Niko. Niko looked unfazed by the entire incident save some red bags under his eyes where he had shed tears. Cawyer was alright. He didn't look or feel injured, and the two arms he had lost earlier had long since grown back.

"Wh—" began Cawyer, but Niko put his forefinger to his lips and said, "Sshh!" The two stood perfectly still.

"Oh, boy," said Tigerstripes. She glanced at her watch. "I may be here a while." She tried to retract into her shell, then remembered she couldn't, being a sea turtle. She sighed as she watched the freshwater turtles frolic about without a care in the world. After about ten minutes of this, the freshwater turtles retracted into their shells. She sighed once more. "Well, I'm an assassin," she said, getting up. "And I guess it's time for me to go finish the job." She mimed rolling up her sleeves and marched down the hill.

Finally, Niko said, "Cawyer, we can talk now. I just clarified that our persistent existence is not a dream!"

Cawyer ran up and caught Niko in a big bear hug. "We're alive!" he shouted. Then, in rapid succession, "We're alive! We're alive! We're alive! We're alive! We're alive! We're alive! We're alive! We're alive! We're alive! We're alive! We're alive! We're alive! We're alive! We're—"

"Yeah, buddy, I think we all get it," said Niko, looking down at the shorter creature and returning the embrace.

"Yes, I think we do," said Tigerstripes.

Cawyer and Niko looked up. "What do you want?!" demanded Cawyer.

"I want your souls!" declared Tigerstripes in an ominous voice. There was silence, and then a chirping sound. "Stupid crickets!" groaned the sea turtle as she stepped on an insect among the grasses.

"Uh, that was a grasshopper," said Niko.

"Crickets are exclusively nocturnal," supplied Cawyer.

Tigerstripes scowled at them like they were the two stupidest people to ever walk the face of the earth. "Oh, really? Thanks for the tip. And, before I kill you two, would either of you be interested in signing a contract suggesting I know nothing of your premature death and am not involved whatsoever in the incident?"

Niko and Cawyer shook their heads.

"Worth a try." She picked up a knife. "Ready?"

Niko and Cawyer looked at each other. They had clearly had enough with all this knife fighting."

They punted her away from them. They turned around and walked on as she landed on her shell into the river with all the freshwater turtles, who scattered at the sight of her (though not very quickly). She could not get out because she had no leverage. Her shell was like a buoy stuck to her back that she could not escape, and her limbs would not reach the river bottom or the shore.

"I will get revenge on those two miscreants," she vowed. "I am not to report back to Cheef and receive the same punishment that Sharpfin did."

CHAPTER 14

Niko and Cawyer walked along. "So, that was fun," said Cawyer.

"What do you mean?!" asked Niko. He looked surprised. "That was horrible! We nearly died!"

"Pffft! Nothing went wrong. We're alive and healthy!"

"You're missing an arm."

"Oh, c'mon! You think anyone's going to notice?"

"Yes."

"Well, I don't."

Far away, hidden among the bracken of the forest, the simian spy took pictures. As he looked at the ones he had just taken, he noticed one of the squid's arms was missing. This was very good. Cheef would be very pleased to see that picture, along with some others he had taken. He couldn't wait to burst Tigerstripes's bubble by showing Cheef photographed proof that she had failed. He ran off.

Some rustling in the bushes could be heard nearby.

"What's that?" asked Niko, whipping his head towards the bushes.

"Which bush did it come from?" asked Cawyer, alarmed.

"I don't know," said Niko, alarmed. They were standing on a narrow path. It was so narrow, in fact, that one was forced to walk in front of the other. However, though the area was considered a prairie, tall grasses and bushes lined everywhere beyond the path. There were two bushes on either side of the part of the path they were standing on.

Cawyer peered inside one bush. "Where are you?" he whispered.

"Right here!" said a voice behind them.

The two twisted around and saw none other than Whiskers the catfish standing behind them.

"What are you doing here?" asked Niko.

"Well, you threw me off that cliff, recall? I decided to make camp in these comforting plains and, what do you know, I found you two here! What a relief! For a second there I thought I'd have to hike back to civilization! And what a task that would've been! I'd have to live off the—"

"Wait, wait, wait," said Cawyer. "Exactly how long would it take to get back to civilization?"

"Nearest rest stop is thirty miles from here."

Niko and Cawyer looked at each other. They had had enough of this guy.

"We'd appreciate it if you left," said Cawyer.

"Yeah, like, right now," added Niko.

"But why?"

"Because you're a pain to have around! We've told you again and again to leave us alone! We've told you constantly that we're not interested in buying stock! But noooooooooo! Of course, you have to be on our trail like a bloodhound and never give up!"

"But I can be more exciting! What if my selling stock became an act in a circus? Would you buy it then?"

Niko and Cawyer put their heads up and imagined what selling stock would look like in a real circus…

"And for our next act," announced a smiling ringmaster, wearing a dapper red suit and top hat, decidedly off-white gloves, and a scholarly mustache and monocle, *"Whiskers Wayne and his amazing 'selling stock' act!"*

A pair of trapeze artists were exiting the ring through a door in the side of it. An elephant carrying Whiskers entered the ring through a door on the opposite side. Whiskers slid off and the elephant exited the ring.

"Heeeeey, kids!" he said. The audience cheered. "For my first feat, I shall do something so daring no one has ever attempted it in a circus ring before! I shall sell stock!" The audience cheered once more. Huzzahs could be heard from every direction. Tables were flipped and roses and orchids thrown in the ring.

"But first," Whiskers continued, "I shall read from my favorite stock market news!" More huzzahs. "Ahem! Article One, Section One, Page One, Paragraph One, Semi-paragraph One! If we give second thought to priori *conversions, then we must take into account lawful mathematics which will…*

Niko and Cawyer shook their heads. It was unthinkable.

"So, are you interested?" asked Whiskers. Niko and Cawyer sighed. "Hey! What?!" shouted Whiskers. Niko and Cawyer picked him up and chucked him as far as they could. Their story continued as they walked along, but to tie up some loose ends that might arise from this single event.

Consequently, the actual story is much larger (and there's some violence involved), but I'll suffice it to say that he crashed into his camp when he landed, destroying the teepee, so he had to rebuild it.

Niko and Cawyer walked along. Soon, they entered a forest. This one was less enjoyable, as the trees were all green and filled with bugs.

"Hey, Niko, do you believe in the theory of relativity?"

"Of course," said Niko.

"What I mean is, do you think it would work at all points?"

"Explain."

"Do you believe the theory of relativity would work underwater?"

"I haven't looked into the science of relativity, so I can't be sure."

"It probably wouldn't. I don't know why I asked such a silly question. Though I do wonder if a compass would work underwater."

"Would be nice if you could ask one of the great scientists of the 19th and 20th centuries such as Issac Newton or Albert Einstein."

"Right. Einstein invented the lightbulb, right?"

"No, Einstein invented the atomic bomb. I believe Thomas Edison invented the lightbulb."

"Did he invent all light-related inventions?"

Niko thought a bit. "You mean like the laser pointer?"

"Speak of the devil…"

"What do you mean?"

Cawyer pointed to the ground.

Niko looked where he was pointing. There was indeed a red dot on the floor. And whoever had thought up the idea for such an invention had created such an ingenious design. Only a red dot appeared on the ground, and there was no beam of light connecting it to the laser pointer it was obviously coming from. That meant the user could be anywhere and they wouldn't know it.

Another ingenious thing about it was that its red color was so visible it would be noticed on the brightest of days and the blackest of nights. The flashlight is not nearly as efficient or bright.

The red dot flitted up to a tree, then down to the ground again, then behind them. They turned around, and the red dot was on the floor in front of the feet of another assassin, who held a laser pointer.

"Hello," said the assassin. And this time, there were two.

CHAPTER 15

Cawyer's eyes went wide.

"Hello," said the assassin again. He grinned, as did his partner. They both had gleaming white sharp teeth, except for the parts where it was yellow.

"We are the Sharp-Toothed Twins," said the smaller one. He was a barracuda. The other was a goblin shark. "And we are here to kill you." Each crossed his fins over their chest and leaned against each other's backs, like hipsters.

"We're not in the mood to get killed today, thank you," said Niko, shielding Cawyer with his arm. "We've had enough of that already lately." He used his gloves to rip the laser pointer from the goblin shark's hands, switch it off, and slip it into his pocket. "So don't even try it." He paused a second. "And, as a side note, how can you two be twins? You're two different species."

"We find loopholes," said the barracuda.

"Oh, we're not going to try to kill you in the way you think," said the goblin shark.

"Huh?" said Cawyer.

"We're too hip, snazzy, and cool to kill brutally."

"Which, for your information, is the way Cheef wants us to kill you," specified the barracuda.

"Who's Cheef?" asked Cawyer.

"Enough!" shouted the goblin shark. The barracuda gave him a look. "Oops. Sorry. Guess I got carried away. But we must be cool!" He cleared his throat. "We shall exterminate you in a tubular way!"

"Tubular?" asked Niko.

"It's hipster slang."

"*Sigh!* Hipsters."

"How would you like to go?"

"What do you mean?"

"How would you like to die? We're going to be cool and allow you to choose."

"Really?" asked Cawyer. "That's quite commendable."

"We're not falling for this!" declared Niko. He blocked Cawyer from walking up to them and then pushed them into a tree.

"We didn't want to have to do this," said the barracuda, groaning. "It's super uncool. But you leave us no choice."

"Didn't want to have to do what?" asked Cawyer.

The goblin shark lunged for them and tackled them, knocking them unconscious.

• • •

It was a long time before they woke up again.

Or so it seemed. Cawyer hoped it hadn't actually been that long.

"Now, tell us how you want to die!" demanded the barracuda's voice.

Cawyer came to his senses and looked around. He came to a surprise. He and Niko were tied tightly to a tree with a vine from one of the trees.

"Well?" asked the barracuda.

"If you don't choose, then we'll be forced to leave you tied to this tree to starve and thirst. We have to kill you somehow, you know. Otherwise, we'll be out of a job!"

"We're not telling you anything!" shouted Niko.

The goblin shark looked genuinely confused. "Why should you?"

"Because you—"

"WE WANT TO BE THROWN OFF A CLIFF!!" shouted Cawyer. Niko looked at him, mouth agape. Cawyer cleared his throat. "We would like to be thrown off a cliff." Then, in a whisper, to Niko, "Trust me."

Niko wasn't so sure.

"Well!" said the barracuda. "I honestly would not have expected something so radical. I expected you to want us to leave you here, where you could die in peace."

"Yeah, me too," said Niko.

"Well, let's get ourselves started," said the goblin shark.

A moment later, Niko and Cawyer were tied to a tree overhanging a cliff face. At the bottom was a rushing river, and the other side wasn't too far away. However, neither was a waterfall.

"Ready to die?" asked the goblin shark.

"Mmm-hmm," said Niko, nodding, though inside he was panicking. Cawyer, on the contrary, appeared collected and composed.

"Sorry it couldn't be a more radical death," said the barracuda. "But we couldn't find a cliff without a river under it."

"Should I begin untying the knots now?" asked the goblin shark.

"No, wait!" said the barracuda. "I think I've got a loose tooth!"

"What's that got to do with anything?"

The barracuda plucked it out. It was as sharp and shiny as a knife. "Use this to cut them loose. It'll be more radical!"

"Good idea!" The goblin shark took the tooth from the barracuda's fin and began to cut Niko and Cawyer loose.

"What is it with these guys and radical stuff?" whispered Cawyer.

"I hope you know what you're doing," whispered Niko. "You might possibly survive, but if I touch the water from this height, it'll be like hitting dry asphalt!"

"Don't worry! I have a plan!"

"I sure hope so."

The goblin shark had almost finished cutting them free. They were now hanging from a single string. "Would you like me to cut this last string? Or would you like me to leave your weight to pull the string?"

"Um..."

"Let their weight finish the job!" shouted the barracuda.

"Okay, I will!" said the goblin shark. He threw the tooth over the edge. Niko and Cawyer watched it fall. It hit a tall rock and split in two. One half was lost among the rocks. One fell into the river and was rushed swiftly away.

"Shall we walk away, hand in hand, laughing at their misfortune?" asked the barracuda.

"We certainly will!" said the goblin shark. They did just that.

"Oh no," said Niko. They were slowly inching closer to certain death. "Please tell me your plan is ready for initiation."

Just a second!" Cawyer wriggled one arm out of the vines, then another. "Okay, I'm ready!"

"Help!" squeaked Niko.

Then they went over the edge.

"WHOAAAAAAAAAAAA!!" they both shouted. Cawyer grabbed one of Niko's arms, then stuck his suckers to the wall. Then he swung and swung and swung, back and forth, gaining momentum. Then, he let go. *Please work*, he silently wished.

Suddenly, they touched down on the cliff's edge, forced to lean forward to avoid falling off again.

"Cawyer, you saved us!" exclaimed Niko. He wrapped him in a big bear hug. "You're my hero!"

"Bigfoot!" said Cawyer, pointing into the woods.

CHAPTER 16

The barracuda and the goblin shark walked through the forest at a leisurely pace.

"Shall we tell Cheef about our success?" suggested the barracuda.

"Of course!" said the goblin shark. "In fact, I think we should suggest him giving us a pizza party in our honor, and employ all his staff to cater it, *and* invite every cool person on the face of the planet!"

"Yeah, yeah, be cool. We'll have to be persuasive."

They soon popped upon the mighty castle. It was really mighty. They uttered the secret knock and ran over the drawbridge inside. Then they ran through the many various halls and ended up in the throne room. Then they burst through the great doors and spoke to the king of the tyrants himself.

"Hey, Cheef!" said the barracuda.

"What's up, buddy?" asked the goblin shark.

"Did you Sharp-Toothed Twins obey my orders and exterminate those varmints?"

"Yeah, we did, King C. And we had a few ideas on how you could reward us for our great feat!" said the goblin shark.

Cheef widened his eyes, clearly surprised. "A fortune in sunglasses and snazzy skateboards isn't enough?"

"Your little gifts are all good, bro," said the barracuda. "But we had something bigger in mind."

Little gifts?! thought Cheef. He was getting angrier on the inside. But he didn't show it on the outside. "What did you have in mind?"

"A pizza party honoring us! Your staff will cater, and every cool person in the world will be invited!"

"Yeah, yeah, I guess I can spare the money for a pizza party. After all, I'll have over fifty times that when this job is finished. I'll give you that reward. Though you will have to give up the sunglasses and skateboards."

The Sharp-Toothed Twins looked between them. This would be a great loss for guys like them. "Can we think about it?" asked the barracuda.

"Take your time," said Cheef, barely holding back a laugh.

"Hooray!" said the goblin shark. The two of them skipped out of the room, arm in arm, cheering.

Now that they were out of the room, Cheef couldn't hold it any longer. He burst out into rapturous laughter. He laughed and laughed and laughed and laughed and laughed. He ho ho ho'd, and ha ha ha'd, and hee hee hee'd. Soon, the great doors of the throne room burst open, meaning his spy had returned from his mission. He wiped away the tears the laughter had resulted in and looked at his employee. "Hello," he said simply.

The spy only nodded, He took out the Polaroids he had taken along the way and held them out to Cheef, who took them.

"I see…" said Cheef, glazing them over. There was one of Tigerstripes disappearing into the forest, one of Niko keeping him and Cawyer safe from certain death by knife with his gloves, and even a particularly humorous one of the Sharp-Toothed Twins luring Niko and Cawyer using a laser pointer.

But two interested him particularly. First there was one of the Sharp-Toothed Twins leaving Niko and Cawyer tied to a tree overhanging a cliff, obviously leaving their own weight to finish the job of sending them plummeting down to the water below. A fine tactic.

If only not one little detail had been ignored.

The next picture was of Cawyer gripping tightly onto the cliff face with his suckers to prevent them from falling to their doom. Then there was a close-up of Niko and Cawyer recovering from the whole ordeal. Strangely, the picture was in high definition, implying that the spy didn't zoom in to take the shot. Interesting...

But that tiny detail... That Niko and Cawyer had survived... That the Sharp-Toothed Twins didn't deserve their stupid reward...

"Spy!" shouted Cheef in anger, throwing all the Polaroids across the room. "Get me the Sharp-Toothed Twins! And send the Crustacean Squad!

• • •

Niko and Cawyer jogged along. The canopy was thicker here, and you couldn't see the sky. They had no time to lose. They had only two hours left to get the gem and get home before Niko was evicted. Hopefully, because the two assassins believed that they were dead, they could continue their journey without interruptions and even take the tiger shark by surprise.

No such luck.

They hadn't even made it five minutes when Whiskers Wayne showed up.

"Again?!" groaned Niko.

"Now, hold on!" said Whiskers. "I now have an entertaining way to sell stock to you!"

"Oh, really?"

"Oh, yes!"

"This better be good.

"*Ahem!* I shall now sell stock to you with balloon animals!"

"?"

Whiskers took out a latex balloon, limp and with no air. Then he blew it up and folded it into a giraffe. He took out and folded three more balloons—one of Whiskers, one of Niko, and one of Cawyer. Before long, he had created a neat little scene with Whiskers holding out his briefcase, Niko and Cawyer both smiling at him, Niko holding out a dollar bill, and a giraffe standing awkwardly off to the side.

"What's this supposed to be?" asked Niko.

"Me selling stock to you boys and you actually liking it!" said Whiskers.

"Seriously?!" asked Cawyer, annoyed.

"I understand my balloon animals are popular at birthday parties! I also attend parties as rare entertainment. My days off are Thursday—"

"Nobody cares!" said Cawyer.

Whiskers reeled back. He had thought Cawyer had a peaceful demeanor.

"What did you say you were popular at?"

"Birthday parties!"

"You just want to swipe some ice cream and skip town!" said Niko.

"Yeah!" said Cawyer.

"What's ice cream?" asked Whiskers innocently.

A little while later, they had him tied to a tree trunk with a vine, facing the balloon animals he had had to watch being popped with a pointy stick. "Where'd you learn this trick of getting rid of people?" asked Whiskers.

"The latest assassin."

"Assassin?"

Niko and Cawyer looked at each other, deciding not to buy it. He had to be an employee of the tiger shark. Maybe not an assassin, but still an employee. It would explain why he showed up after every assassin.

And, as we all know, directly before the next.

As soon as they were out of sight of Whiskers, they heard a bunch of clicking noises, as if someone was playing castanets. There was one that was distinguished from the others by a lower pitch.

"I'm afraid to turn around," said Niko.

But they did.

"Oh no," said Cawyer. A king crab was sitting there, amongst a crowd of crabs clicking their claws.

CHAPTER 17

"Now what?! asked Cawyer in an exasperated voice.

The king crab stepped forward. "I am King Augustus Crab, supreme ruler of the Crustacean Squad!"

"Yeah, I can see that," muttered Niko.

"We are here to kill you!"

"Again?"

"There were people before us?"

"Yes."

"Dang it all! I thought we would be the first in history to accomplish such a task!"

"Well, either you will, or you'll be the last," said Cawyer.

"Yeah, because no one's accomplished killing us, but they sure have accomplished trying to!" exclaimed Niko.

"You can accomplish being the first ones to die at our hand!" said Cawyer.

King Augustus frowned. "I'd rather not. It would be a shameful thing to be remembered by."

"At least you wouldn't be there to suffer the humiliation."

The king crab held out a gnarled, giant claw towards Niko and Cawyer. "First wave of attack!" he shouted. "Contact!"

"Contact!" came some combined voices within the crowd of crusty crustaceans.

"What's going on?" Cawyer whispered to Niko,

"I don't know," Niko whispered back. "But it doesn't look good."

Suddenly, out of nowhere, about twelve lobsters charged out of the army and clamped their claws around their ankles. Niko yowled with pain. Cawyer didn't feel much because of his rubbery skin and lack of touch sensors, but he fell to the ground because the lobsters had rendered his legs useless.

In the background, at the back of the army, three fiddler crabs began to play a tune with their fiddle-like claws.

Eventually, they removed the lobsters. The lobsters snarled at them, then dove in for another attack. Niko and Cawyer shielded their faces and waited for the inevitable.

Suddenly, a lobster trap sprang out of the trees above them. It was held by a string and swinging towards them. The lobsters paused their pursuit, ducking to avoid the swinging trap. It missed them altogether. "Hah!" said one of the lobsters. "I guess your defense mechanism didn't work! Now we'll carry on with our work."

"That wasn't us," said Niko.

The lobster trap, meanwhile, had to obey the laws of physics, so it swung back towards the lobsters and scooped them up, carrying them up into the treetops. Everyone, even Niko and Cawyer, gaped in disbelief.

But the happiness was not about to last.

"Second wave!" shouted King Augustus, and three hairy blue crabs, each twice the size of a lobster, charged towards them.

"What are they going to do, brush against us?" Niko scoffed.

"Never underestimate the ability of blue crabs," Cawyer whispered.

They weren't planning to brush against them, in fact. Two climbed up Niko's body. Niko tried to brush them off his shirt, but they held fast. One landed on his neck and stretched its claw to pinch his nose, which gave Niko extreme pain.

The other climbed on top of Niko's head, stretched their claws downwards, and pinched his ears.

"Yeow!" shouted Niko, desperately trying to pry the crabs off his face.

The last one, who climbed up Cawyer's body, did not have a nose or ears to pinch, so he did what any crab would do and went for the limbs.

The crab opened up his giant, hairy, sharp claw, and began to cut. He secured his claw around one of Cawyer's arms and snipped. The arm fell to the ground like the end of a string that was cut. Seven arms to go. He snipped the next arm off, then moved up.

"Niko!" shouted Cawyer. "Help me! The crab is snipping my arms off!"

"AAAAAAHHHHH!" was all Niko could say. Things were not at their finest in this moment.

However, an arm holding a snow shovel popped out of the trees. The arm was short, though it had a long sleeve and a glove, making it unidentifiable.

It pried the crabs from Niko and Cawyer's faces and scooped them up in the process. Then it carried them into the leaves. Unusually, they made no outcry. Now, as Niko realized, the lobsters didn't either.

Then they heard it.

Screaming, coming from the crabs. Niko and Cawyer couldn't see what was happening, but it seemed the crabs already knew what was going on.

"They're boiling our numbers alive!!" shouted King Augustus.

"Should we scream and run around in circles?" asked one of the crabs.

"Try and see if you can. But crabs can only scream if ultimate suffering is upon them. Such as being boiled alive for instance."

"Or the death of a loved one?" suggested Cawyer.

The king scoffed. "Love? Oh, please! We crustaceans are beyond such emotions!"

Cawyer gasped.

"But I suppose you must die." Then he cleared his throat and bellowed, "Third wave!"

An army of shrimp gladiators came running. Their spears drawn, their shields at their chests, and their Viking-helmeted leader leading them into battle.

But they didn't.

"Aw, look at the tiny shrimps running around in their cute gladiator costumes!" exclaimed Cawyer.

"They're not costumes!" shouted the chief. "They're real!" It was a deep bellow, but to Niko and Cawyer it sounded like a high-pitched shriek, barely a sound. The shrimp were only two inches high, after all.

"Get them!" shouted the leader. Every soldier picked up a bucket of krill, tiny, partly parasitic crustaceans, cousins of shrimp. They were nearly microscopic to humans, but not to shrimp! "Get him, tiger," one soldier whispered to his bucket. They all launched their contents in the air, spilling their contents on the enemy's feet.

At first, Niko didn't feel anything. But as the krill crawled up his legs, it was like lice on his skin instead of his hair. He itched his legs like crazy, and then his hips…

Cawyer, meanwhile, didn't have trouble. His lack of touch sensors didn't allow him to itch. The krill decided to burrow into his skin and infect him instead, but they found he didn't even have cartilage, let alone bones!

"Worst body ever!" shouted one krill.

It looked like the end. But then, what do you know it, three crab pots fell from the trees, hanging by threads, far behind the army of crabs, who anticipated the disaster Niko and Cawyer were facing with glee. One crab looked behind him and said, "Look out!"

Too late. By the time the crabs had turned around, the crab pots were already on them, scooping them into the trees and the same awful fate the other crabs had met.

Even King Augustus was not immune. "I'll get you two for this!" he shouted. Then the same short arm sprayed some pesticides down, killing the shrimp and krill.

Nothing moved.

"That was… odd," remarked Niko.

CHAPTER 18

Niko and Cawyer walked along.

"Who was helping us?" asked Niko.

"Well, I don't know about you…" said Cawyer, "…but I'm willing to just let it be. At least we got out of there alive!"

"I know, but I still wonder. I mean, who would go to the trouble to save us? We were going to be killed. It would have to be someone who cares about us…"

"…or at least cares about keeping us alive…"

"…but why?"

Cawyer shrugged. "Maybe it's another assassin who wanted to take the credit for killing us instead of those crabs."

Niko thought a moment. "I think you're right, Cawyer. It's the solution that makes the most sense, after all."

"GREETINGS!!" cheered a voice that Niko and Cawyer felt was familiar but couldn't see yet.

"Who are you?!" shouted Cawyer.

"I am Dr. Wayne II," said a formal catfish with a monocle. "Please let me take you to your table."

"Table?"

"Of course, my good man! Do you not realize you are in my outdoor restaurant?"

"Outdoor restaurant?" Niko echoed.

"*In* it?" wondered Cawyer aloud.

Pretty soon, they came to a giant and perfectly splendid dining room. It was the first view of the sky they had had in a while. There were hundreds of tables, each with a pink tablecloth, two chairs, and a beautiful ornate vase with a few roses inside. And even though there didn't seem to be any people at the diner, there was a stage for dinner theater.

"Wow," said Niko. "This place is amazing!"

"Thank you very much," said Dr. Wayne, seating them at a table. "A waitress will take your orders shortly. And don't forget to applaud for dinner theater!"

"Don't worry, we won't!"

Dr. Wayne smiled and walked through a door into the kitchen.

"Boy, the atmosphere in here really is something, isn't it?" asked Cawyer, smiling.

"I don't know," said Niko. "I have an uneasy feeling about this place."

"Oh, c'mon, Niko! Loosen up! You're at a possible five-star restaurant to grab a quick lunch before heading off to make your fortune! What could possibly go wrong?"

Just then, a catfish in heavy makeup, blonde curly hair, and an elegant scarlet dress walked up to them. "What can I get you boys?" "she" asked them. The voice sounded falsetto.

"I'll take… uh…" Cawyer trailed off. He found there weren't any menus!

"Silly me!" said the waitress. She handed them a couple menus and two glasses of water and walked away.

As they sipped on the water, Niko and Cawyer looked in distaste at all the food on the menu.

A few minutes later, the waitress returned. "Anything strike your fancy, boys?"

"Yeah, uh, I've realized all you have on the menu is inedible food."

"Wha...?" asked the waitress in genuine confusion.

"It's all crabs!"

"Not true! There's some lobsters and shrimp."

"Is there anything that isn't crustaceans?"

"There's sea slugs."

"Ew!" exclaimed Cawyer. "I'll stick with my water, thanks."

"I think I'll get a shrimp cocktail."

"Okay!" said the waitress. She wrote down their orders and returned to the kitchen.

"Is it just me?" asked Niko. "Or is something seriously off about this place?"

"Like what?" asked Cawyer. "It's a beautiful experience!"

"Well, for one, everyone working here seems to be a catfish."

"That's just a coincidence!"

"Secondly, the menu is mainly crab after we had just fought an army of crabs who were boiled alive."

"That's just circumstantial!"

"Someone is definitely onto us," said Niko. He knelt his head toward Cawyer and kept his voice down so no one else could hear. "Think of it. Every assassin or group of assassins we've seen so far has had one goal: kill us. And out of all of them, only the crabs died.

The others simply walked off. One of them must have cooked them alive and sold them to this restaurant for an extra buck."

"What are the facts?"

"Well, the assassins must be listed. First, Sharpfin. He ran off into the woods after chopping down that tree and nearly killing us. He also announced he would return. He could be here any second now! Of course, then again, there's Tigerstripes. She just disappeared, didn't she?"

"Well, no. We kicked her into a pond, remember?"

"Oh, yes. How could I forget? Well, anyhow, she could have escaped and is now aiming to get her revenge. This could be her moment! We must also take into account the fact that both could have killed the crabs for the same motive: ruining their chance to kill us forever and giving them another chance. And I'll bet this time they won't be so merciful. No, no, no. They'll try to kill us until the two possible outcomes: they die or we do."

"That's heartless."

"Of course it is! Now, all I'm saying is that we need to be on guard. Keep an eye open for abnormal activity."

"What about the Sharp-Toothed Twins?"

"The goblin shark and the barracuda? They walked off thinking they'd killed us, remember? They probably went to their boss to finish the job by telling them they'd won."

"But the crabs wouldn't have come if—"

"HELLO!" said a gleeful, familiar voice.

Niko and Cawyer snapped to attention. They knew the bearer of that voice.

"Whiskers?!" Cawyer shouted up to the top hat-wearing catfish on the stage. "What are you doing up there?!"

"Performing, of course! I'm the entertainment!"

Niko and Cawyer slumped in their seats. "This was the entertainment?"

"The restaurant's management must be cracked."

"For my first act, I will pull a bunny out of my hat!"

"This ought to be good."

"Ta-da!"

Niko and Cawyer snapped to attention once more. Whiskers was holding an origami bunny made from the latest newspaper. "I don't get it," said Cawyer.

"But you will!" Whiskers unfolded the bunny and checked one of the articles. "Let's see how the stock market reports are doing today."

"EURGH!" shouted Niko. "Get it through your head! We don't want to buy stock! We will never want to buy stock!"

"Niko! He's gone!"

"What?" While Niko was shouting, he didn't realize that Whiskers had walked off. "Well, let's leave anyway! I don't want to spend another second in this place!"

"I'm with you!"

They walked off just as Whiskers, posing as the waitress, came through the door of the kitchen and hollered, "Your shrimp cocktail is ready!" She screamed, "Oh!" when it suddenly flew out of her hand and into the forest.

CHAPTER 19

"Mmm!" exclaimed Niko as he and Cawyer walked off. He was dipping his shrimp in his cocktail sauce and chewing it up, spitting out the ends. "I'm glad I was able to swipe this."

"Yes, your gloves certainly are revolutionary," answered Cawyer.

WHUMP! WHUMP!

"Uh, Cawyer? Was that you?"

"No!"

WHUMP!

"Oh no! Another assassin! This is horrible!"

"Relax! It's probably the last one."

"How can you be sure?"

"The compass is still giving me power!"

"The compass?! You still have the compass?! After all this time?!"

"Yes! It's the one thing I managed to hold onto throughout all these hardships. How do you think we knew the right way to walk?"

"I-I don't know!"

WHUMP! WHUMP! "I'm coming for you!" came a deep voice.

"Oh no!" Niko shrieked. He began to run in the other direction. Come with me, Cawyer! We must live!" He began to climb one of the trees.

"No, Niko! We must fight!"

"Can't you hear how amazingly huge he is?!"

"I'm coming for you!"

"On second thought…" Cawyer began to climb the tree as well.

Suddenly, the giant creature burst through the bracken before them. It was a walrus. "I'm still coming for you!" it bellowed.

"RUN!!" screamed Niko. He and Cawyer burst their heads above the canopy. Here, the sun shone brightly, though it was, unfortunately, an afternoon sun. They both propelled themselves above the leaves and ran in the direction the compass was pointing, only this time above the forest instead of through it. It was just like running through a grassy field, except for—

"AUGH!" shouted Cawyer. He fell through a gap in the trees. He would have fallen to the floor if Niko hadn't grabbed the end of his arm just in time. "Help!"

"I've got you!" said Niko. Above the trees felt like home, though the gaps in the trees felt like windows into the underworld. He tried to pull Cawyer up, but he was caught on something. "Cawyer! What are your tentacles caught on?!"

"Me!" said the deep voice. The walrus could not climb trees, but now that Cawyer had fallen, he could easily reach up and pull him down. Niko was the only thing stopping him. "I shall chop you into calamari!"

"NIKO, PLEASE!!"

"I've got you!"

"Mine!" The walrus jerked hard on Cawyer's tentacles, causing both him and Niko to fall to the ground. After some groaning, they looked up and beheld their enemy. The walrus loomed over them menacingly. "Now you die!"

"Admit it!" cried Cawyer. "Who sent you?!"

The walrus chuckled and cracked his knuckles. "That will not be necessary." He then jumped as high as he could in the air and landed on them. His bulky mass easily squished them like a bug. "Are you dead yet?" he asked.

No answer.

"Maybe I ought to check on them, make sure they're okay." He lifted his body off of them and beheld what remained of Niko and Cawyer. It was a flat picture, with both characters' faces contorted in pain. The walrus laughed heartily. Then he stopped. "How did I do this? Doesn't this stuff only happen in cartoons?"

"You're right, it does!" came a voice from the flattened failure.

"Huh? Who said that?"

"Us!" Niko and Cawyer burst up from the ground.

"What? How did this happen?"

"Well, we escaped, and that flattened thing is only body paint you had on before it rubbed off on the ground," said Cawyer.

"How did you escape?!"

"This guy used his gloves to quickly dig a tunnel we squeezed into that your flabby mass couldn't reach into."

"And now I'll use them on you!" exclaimed Niko. He forced power from his gloves towards the walrus.

But it had no effect.

"Oh no, he's immune!" shouted Cawyer.

"We're dead!" gulped Niko.

The walrus guffawed. "You losers have even admitted that you are as good as dead at my hands already!"

Niko suddenly stiffened. With one arm he held Cawyer's arm. "Not today, pinniped!" he declared. Then he pushed down towards the ground with his gloves and lifted him and Cawyer into the sky.

"No!" shouted the walrus.

"Ha, ha, you lose!" shouted Cawyer.

Niko and Cawyer soon landed on the treetops. "C'mon!" said Niko. They ran as fast as they could. There were no pitfalls, and the trees completely covered their view of the ground and the fast-pursuing walrus' view of them.

"Come back!" shouted the walrus, huffing and puffing below them.

"Sorry, you snooze, you lose!" shouted Cawyer.

"You know, we need a way to get rid of him!" said Niko.

"Why?"

Suddenly, they stopped. Before them was the edge of the tree line, and even farther on was a strange structure.

"What do we do?" asked Cawyer.

"We—"

"Come down here!" shouted the walrus, cutting Niko off. He was looking up at them.

"Never!" said Cawyer. "We'll never come down!"

"Well, you may want to reconsider." He cracked his flabby knuckles, then shook the tree Niko and Cawyer were standing on violently with his strong arms.

"Oh no!"

The tree cracked and swayed.

"Oh no, Niko! We're dead!"

"Oh, no we're not!" Niko gripped the tree's branches tightly and told Cawyer to do the same. They held on throughout the entire two-minute-long situation.

Suddenly, the tree's trunk gave way, and the two friends toppled over. "Change position!" shouted Niko. They inched backwards, down the side of the tree trunk that was exposed to the air so they wouldn't feel too much impact. A scream and a grunt were heard.

"What was that?!" exclaimed Cawyer.

"That guy," said Niko. He pointed to the walrus, who had been flattened by the tree. "Poor flabby fellow was too fat and slow to evacuate in time."

"Hooray!"

"I wouldn't cheer yet, Cawyer."

"Why?"

Niko pointed to the dark, stone brick structure before them. It was undoubtedly the tiger shark's base.

CHAPTER 20

It was a horrible thing to look at, oh yes it was. The dark structure looked like death itself. The stone material obviously hated nature. And the moat of lava surrounding it totally wrecked the underwater theme!

"What do we do?" Cawyer asked nervously.

"We do what we did with everything else," said Niko. "Charge in headfirst and never look back!"

"I'm with you!"

They charged towards the dark structure. Eventually they reached the moat. "How do we get to the other side?" asked Cawyer.

"There!" said Niko, pointing. There was a drawbridge on the other side. Drawn, of course.

"I doubt they'll let that down for us."

"Is there any other way?"

"Hmm…"

Just then, Whiskers stepped into their line of vision. "Hello."

"Don't interact with him," Niko said. "I have an idea." He brought out the laser pointer and aimed it at the ground. Whiskers jolted to attention. Niko slowly moved the laser across the floor and into the lava, where Whiskers jumped after it.

"We've seen the last of him," said Cawyer.

Just then, a familiar voice sprouted from the lava moat. "There's only one way!"

"Which is?"

"To fight me!"

Niko and Cawyer looked down. There was Tigerstripes, sitting on a large rock in the lava. She was holding a black bo stick. She pressed a button that was mysteriously there. Obviously, the rock was synthetic, because it split up into five divided, thin platforms that rose into the sky and stood suspended there. Tigerstripes was able to grab one and hurl herself onto it. She sat exactly in the center. She was on the side of the moat closest to the castle, and Niko and Cawyer were on the other. "I challenge you to a rematch!" she declared.

Cawyer scoffed. "A rematch? Really? Hey, how come no one else came to the party?"

"They were all executed upon returning, I suppose."

Niko threw a pebble onto a platform. The platform didn't give out. "Are these safe to walk on?" he asked. "I mean, what's holding them up?"

"Magnetism. It's very complicated. Let's just say that the minerals and metals in the walls of this moat are creating a negative magnetic force towards the platforms, pushing them away. However, this force can only go so far, so the platforms are stuck right here."

"I don't trust you!" said Niko. "We'll find some other way across this moat!"

"Okay, but it's forty miles in diameter…"

"Well, we're not going to get to that building standing here," said Cawyer. He walked on top of the nearest platform. However, it began to tip. His suckers gripped the platform. The platform tipped upside-down, with Cawyer hanging from the underside.

"Oh, did I forget to mention?" asked Tigerstripes. "The platforms will tip over with the slightest weight." She smiled deviously.

"You set this up just to kill us!" shouted Niko.

Tigerstripes smiled wider.

"Niko, I know how we can get out of this mess!" said Cawyer.

"How?"

"I will be the balancing agent. You will make your way across the platforms and toward the end above them, I will do the same below them. We'll each walk in synchronized locations on each platform. When you cross to the next, I will as well!"

"Cawyer, that's an excellent plan!"

"Aw, shucks."

Tigerstripes struck a ninja pose with her bo stick. "I will ensure that you do not reach the end!"

"Oh no!" said Cawyer.

"We'll push through!" said Niko. He began to run.

There was a systematic order of things. Niko hopped onto the same platform Cawyer was hanging off. They both took steps exactly where the other one did. When Niko stepped carefully onto the next platform, Cawyer did the same. Cawyer even tripped and slipped once (it is not easy to hang off the bottom of a platform), and Niko had to copy that, a very risky move.

But Tigerstripes was too much for them. She would quickly move from one platform to another. Her quick movements meant she would never capsize it. She would also ruin their efforts by jabbing at Niko with her bo stick. He could get out of the way just fine and still maintain balance when she struck for his head or chest, thus Cawyer wouldn't need to replicate the movements. But when she struck for his ankles to try and trip him, he would have to jump back. This was where it got tricky.

Tigerstripes made a quick jab for Niko's ankles. Niko whispered, "Jump!", his and Cawyer's code for jumping back. Niko jumped backwards and onto the next platform. Cawyer moved backwards to the same platform in the exact same spot as fast as he could, all in a split second.

Tigerstripes snarled. She lunged for Niko, causing him to jump back again. Niko decided it was time to fight back. He pushed her to the other side of the moat, and he and Cawyer walked together as fast as they could.

Tigerstripes landed far back. She quickly moved to the next platform so she wouldn't fall into the inferno below.

"Whew!" exclaimed Niko, wiping his brow. "It's hot here."

"How is she so fast?" asked Cawyer. "Aren't turtles supposed to be slow?

"You're thinking of tortoises."

"Hi-yah!" shouted Tigerstripes. She hopped off her platform and towards Niko. She pushed him backwards and landed on the platform behind him. When she looked back, he was gone. "Hah! There he goes. And that stupid squid couldn't possibly find his way back up! I win! Hah! Now I'll go and get my reward." She walked into the dark structure.

Little did she know...

"Cawyer, you saved me!" said Niko. He and Cawyer were holding hands. Cawyer's feet were firmly planted on the underside of the platform.

"Get ready!" said Cawyer.

"Get ready for whaaaAAAAAAAAAAA?!" Cawyer swung Niko up to the platform. Niko steadied himself, then they both moved briskly across the platforms and into the building.

There were giant double doors, and though they looked intimidating, they could easily be opened with some elbow grease.

They sped through the hall, paying very little attention to the decorations, and came to the next room.

"Ha wha bla blee bloopie bla," babbled Cawyer.

"Homina, homina, homina," said Niko.

They were looking at a giant maze of cars and trucks, some even from foreign countries. There were pizza trucks, mini vans, sports cars, tractors, bicycles, and even the engine and a car of a freight train.

"How do we navigate to the other side?" asked Cawyer.

"We—" began Niko, but Cawyer clamped the end of his arm over his mouth. "Look!" he whispered.

Tigerstripes was navigating the maze.

"Let's get her," said Niko.

They snuck up behind her. Cawyer tapped her shoulder. She spun around. "Oh, hello," she said in a nervous voice.

They threw her out onto one of the platforms. She was off-balance, so she tipped into the molten liquid below shell-first. Though she was floating on the surface, the shell could only withstand so much. It slowly sank into the lava. "HELP!!" she screamed. "AAAAUGH! AAAAAAAAAAAAAAAAAAAUGH!!!"

Niko and Cawyer smiled. Then they heard a, "Hey, you!" They spun around. A guard in a gorilla suit had spotted them.

CHAPTER 21

"What is your business here?" the guard demanded. He was holding a sharp battle axe.

Niko and Cawyer looked at each other and decided it was best not to comment on the situation. They ran past the guard and tore through the maze.

"Hey, get back here!" the guard shouted, running after them.

Niko and Cawyer stopped. "We need a new strategy," said Niko.

"Why?" asked Cawyer. "We're getting away from that ape just fine."

"Apes can't talk! And besides, apes have longer arms than legs. That guy didn't!"

Cawyer shrugged. "Maybe it was Bigfoot." Then he gasped. "Niko, I know—"

"Hold that thought." Niko looked up the side of a school bus and scratched his chin. Then he spun his head around and looked behind them. The guard was advancing fast. "I have an idea," he said. "It will get us out of this maze faster."

"I'll try anything."

"I'll need your cooperation."

"Anything."

"Can you boost me up the side of this school bus?"

Cawyer looked up. "No. Can you boost me?"

"Sure, why not?"

"I'm coming for you!" shouted the guard.

"Hurry!" said Cawyer. Niko boosted him up.

"Now pull me up!" said Niko. Cawyer pulled him up.

The guard came into view. "Now I've got you!" he said. "Hey, how'd you get up there?!"

"Run!" shouted Niko. He and Cawyer sprinted across the tops of the vehicles. Pizza trucks, city buses, supercars, taxicabs, and even submarines. All got hopped upon by the fleeing friends.

"I can see the end!" said Cawyer.

"Naturally," said Niko.

They hopped off the last truck and towards the giant double doors, still ten yards ahead of the guard. They opened them with some difficulty and made their way into the hall on the other side.

The guard came into view. "Hey, stop right—" was all he could get out before they shut the doors and locked them.

"Phew," said Cawyer.

"Catch your breath," said Niko.

After five seconds of deep breaths, they noticed that there were two sleeping guards near them who hadn't woken up during the whole ordeal. They both gasped, then covered their mouths quickly.

"How do we get past them?" asked Cawyer.

Niko pointed to a vent cover. He mimed pulling it off.

Cawyer got the message. He tried to give Niko a thumbs-up, but he didn't have any thumbs. "Why don't we just walk along the hall?"

"We risk attracting more guards."

Niko crawled to the vent cover. It was ground-level. There was a guard sleeping right next to it. Niko cautiously took the compass they had managed to hang onto for so long, smashed the glass shielding its face, and broke the needle off.

"WHAT THE HECK'D YOU DO THAT FOR?!" Cawyer whisper-yelled, which, in my opinion, is just as loud as talking normally.

"We don't need it anymore," whispered Niko. "We're in the castle."

Niko used the needle as a screwdriver head to pry the screws off the vent cover. Then he slipped the needle in his pocket, should it prove useful later, and Cawyer crawled through the vent. He motioned for Niko to follow.

They crawled silently through the vents. They went up once, confirming that they were now at roof level. Eventually they reached a dip in the landscape. "Eh?" said Cawyer.

"What is it?" asked Niko. He couldn't see because he was behind Cawyer.

"The tunnel ends here horizontally, but it goes downwards."

"So? Let's just climb down!"

"No! There's a high-powered fan here. Right below it is a vent cover that leads to who-knows-where."

"Why?!"

Cawyer shrugged. "Got to have decent air conditioning in a place surrounded by a moat of lava."

"Hmmmm... I know! We'll lodge something in the fan so it stops spinning! Then we'll climb under it safely and go through the vent cover."

"Good idea."

Niko handed him the compass needle he had. Cawyer threw it as hard as he could into the spinning fan, and it jammed the blades. There was a great sound of grinding metal. "I hope no one heard that."

They climbed through the vent cover and fell a height of seven feet to the floor. "Oof," said Niko. Suddenly, the sound of grinding metal was heard again. The compass needle fell to the floor and the fan resumed spinning. Niko picked it up and put it in his pocket.

"Let's go," said Cawyer.

"Where to?"

"Well, this looks like the place. Their chief probably lives here."

The plaque above the giant double doors read, "CHEEF". "Yeah, but poorly spelled."

"Hide!" Cawyer pushed Niko into a corridor. This corridor led to the armory.

"What was that for?"

There's an army of guards. They must have been on break or something, but they've returned, and they're guarding the door."

"Well, what do we do about it?"

Cawyer glanced in the direction of the various gorilla suits and spears. He smiled. "I may have an idea."

A moment later, Niko and Cawyer were walking out of the armory in gorilla suits. It was comfortable for Niko. It fit him perfectly. But for Cawyer, who had four times the amount of arms and an oddly shaped head, it was stiff and uncomfortable, for he had to make it fit best he could. He waddled around.

They walked towards the giant double doors. Once they got there, a guard held out his hand in the universal sign for "STOP!" and grunted. Niko pointed to the entrance. The guard nodded and allowed them to pass, but they arose his suspicions when he saw Cawyer waddling awkwardly.

Once Niko and Cawyer were in, they removed their gorilla suits. They were inside the belly of the beast.

"Okay, just keep a low profile, all right?" said Niko as Cawyer wiggled out of his suit with some difficulty. "With any luck, we—"

"Hello," said a voice.

Niko and Cawyer looked up. Sitting there menacingly on his throne was the dreaded tiger shark.

"Guards!" the shark called out.

"Oh no!" said Cawyer. Guards began to enter the room.

"Nice try," said the shark. "I am Cheef, the most powerful tiger shark in the WORLD!" That last word echoed against the walls of the room. The room's ceiling was twelve feet high. "Now you shall die here knowing that you failed on your journey, fools!"

CHAPTER 22

"Fools?" echoed Niko. He would not take it. After coming so far, he would not lose his chance!

He looked behind him and saw the approaching guards. Determined and angry, he pushed them back as hard as he could with his gloves. "Whoa!" they shouted. He pushed them out the door.

Cheef's eyes went wide. "Impressive!" his voice boomed. "But let's see if you can handle this!" He leaped off his throne and landed on the floor. He charged towards Niko, picked him up, and threw him across the room.

Cawyer's eyes flitted to a door at the other side of the room, but he quickly refocused them to the scene, afraid that Cheef would notice him eyeing the only available exit and post some guards to it.

Cheef turned his attention to Cawyer. Cawyer gulped. Cheef reached his fin out to grab him. Cawyer yelped and ran off in the direction of the exit. Cheef chased after him.

Meanwhile, Niko noticed something. There was a keyhole just sitting there randomly on the wall. He quickly looked around to make sure Cawyer was still occupying Cheef's attention and took the compass needle out of his pocket and used it to pick the lock. It gave way to a room built into the wall panels. Niko gasped at what was inside the wall.

Cawyer ran through the door he saw earlier. The door was too small for Cheef to enter, so all he did was bang against the door.

Cawyer took a few deep breaths, then he turned around. What he saw took his breath away. The gorilla spy that had been following them through the forest, the one Cawyer had mistaken for Bigfoot, was standing there wide-eyed looking at Cawyer with a camera in his hand.

Niko walked into the compartment. He felt the gem with his hands. "How amazing," he said. "I've never seen it in my life, yet it joys me greatly to be reunited with it."

"But not for long!" said Cheef. He snuck up behind Niko and grabbed him.

"ACK!" Niko yelped.

"Nice try. But I'm going to use this for a highly specific laser that will aid surgeons in amazing medical operations, which will make much more profit than simply selling it. And now you die!" said Cheef.

"Help!" said Cawyer. Cheef spun his head around to see. The spy kicked Cawyer out of the room, reentered, and locked the door. Cawyer desperately jiggled the handle. "No no no!" shouted Cawyer. "Open up!"

Cheef grinned. He tossed Niko to the side and started for Cawyer. "No!" shouted Niko. He looked around for something he could use as a weapon and his eyes fell upon the crystal. "Hmm…"

Cheef picked Cawyer up. "Say goodbye, fool!" he said.

"Hey, you!" said Niko. Cheef spun his head around. Niko was holding up the heavy jewel with his powers. Cheef gasped. "Brace yourself!" Niko spun around and whacked Cheef in the jaw. Cheef fell to the ground, stunned. Cawyer wiggled free.

"Niko, you're a genius!"

"Come with me! We're not out of this yet, and there's no time to lose!"

The two of them ran as fast as they could out of the room and through the halls. The rabble of guards that they met earlier spotted them and gave chase. "Get back here!" they shouted.

"Catch us if you can!" said Cawyer.

Once they reached the exit, they tripped over the feet of the guards they saw even earlier, awakening them. "Hey!" they said.

"Too late!" said Cawyer. He and Niko escaped through the exit and into the maze of cars.

"Quick!" said Niko. "We're running out of time!"

"What do we do? It'd take forever to go across the platforms without dying."

"Into this car!" said Niko. He pulled Cawyer through the doors of a '90s pizza truck and popped the gem in the trunk.

"What are we going to do?!" The sound of the approaching guards became louder.

"I'll tell you what we're going to do," said Niko. He took the compass needle out of his pocket once more and twisted it in the keyhole.

The engine roared to life and the car began rumbling.

"That's amazing, Niko! Your needle has so many uses!"

"GET BACK HERE!" shouted Cheef, who was making his way through the crowd of guards.

"Let's go!" said Niko. He floored the gas pedal and sped out of the maze. He twisted and turned until he reached one of those trucks with a ramp attached to the back. He went up it and began to speed over the cars instead of through them.

"Hey, I came up with a perfect tongue twister! 'Niko's needle negates nautical nefariousness'!"

"That is pretty good."

"OVER HERE!" shouted Cheef, riding after them on a BMX.

"Whoa!"

"Hurry!" They rode across the platforms above the moat easily and out into the world.

They sped through the green forest. Past the site of the outdoor restaurant. Into the field where they had fought Tigerstripes. "We're going to make it!"

They stopped at the base of the waterfall. "What are we going to do now?" asked Cawyer.

Suddenly, a large hook on a cable dove down toward them. It latched onto the fender and slowly reeled itself back in, bringing them with it.

"What's happening?" asked Cawyer.

The car landed on top of the cliff. Gazing out the windshield, Niko saw Percy in front of them. "I knew you would need help."

"We've won!" said Cawyer.

But it wasn't meant to be. They drove a little too close to the curb and hit a stop sign, which blocked their windshield and their view, eventually resulting in them ramming into a fire hydrant and it spraying water all over. "I hate stop signs," Niko muttered.

Suddenly, Cheef appeared. "I'm coming for you!" he shouted.

"Oh no!" shouted Cawyer.

"Bail out!" shouted Niko. He and Cawyer fled the pizza truck with the gem.

"Wait! No!!" Cheef couldn't stop the BMX, and it crashed into the pizza truck.

A few hours later...

Cheef sleepily blinked his eyes open. "Wha... What happened?"

"Oh, good you're awake," said Cawyer. "The doctors were getting worried."

"What the—" He was lying in a hospital bed with casts and bandages all over his body. "No! No!!!"

"Well, when you crashed, we got doctors to help you. We also got police to arrest you and all your little ape henchmen. Your spy got away, though."

"All of Niko's rent is paid off and he is now making money as an inventor!"

"Hooray!"

"No! NO! NOOOOOOOOOOOOOOOO!!!!!!!!!!!"

They left the hospital room with high spirits. "I'm pretty sure we made everybody proud today," said Cawyer.

"Are you kidding? Nobody knew we went on that adventure! Heck, hardly anyone in this town knows we exist!"

"We made the news when we crashed into that fire hydrant."

Niko gave him a serious look.

"Well, I'm proud of us."

"Ditto."

As they were walking, they saw Whiskers on the street. "What are you doing here?" asked Niko.

"I narrowly avoided death by landing on one of the platforms suspended above the lava," said Whiskers.

"So you were never working for Cheef?"

"No." Whiskers walked away.

"I'm glad to know that," said Niko.

"Me too," agreed Cawyer.

They smiled at each other and walked off into the sunset.

THE END

ABOUT THE AUTHOR

Alexander Dubbels lives in Plainview, Minnesota, USA. He has been writing for years, but this is his first published work. He has four siblings, one of which has written two books and one who keeps starting one but has never gotten around to finishing it. He loves looking at trees of many colors and writing about them.

COMING SOON

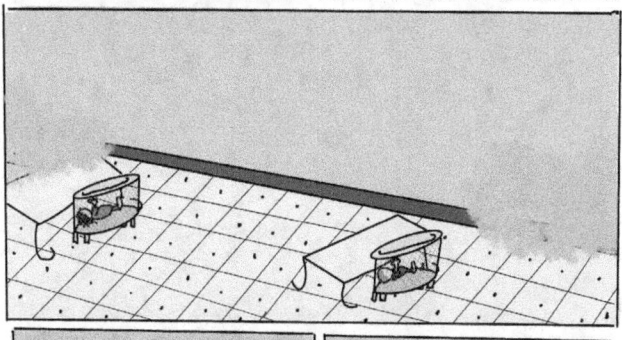